A DOOR
NEVER OPENED

A DOOR

NEVER OPENED

©

The Sequel to the Scholarly Novel

"In a World We Never Made"

DANIEL HILL ZAFREN

Time Treasures Books
Books treasured for all time

Copyright © 2003 by Daniel Hill Zafren

Originally published by Beard Books
Republished in 2006 by Time Treasures Books,
Charlotte, North Carolina

ISBN 13: 978-0-9778892-2—8
ISBN 10: 0-9778892-2-X

Printed in the United States of America

Cover image is from the limited print *The Blue Door* by Douglas Grier, Edisto Island, South Carolina, and is used with the permission and by the courtesy of the artist.

The poems by Glenn Logan, *Less and More* and *One & One*, are used with the permission of the poet.

To the memory of my father, Gilbert
Zafren, a gentle man of peace, fair-
ness, and understanding. He garnered respect and admiration from
all fortunate enough to know him.
His original poems to my mother are
the framework upon which
this book is built;

and also

To my loving wife, Valarie, whose
constant support snd encouragement make all of my accomplishments possible.

Footfalls echo in the memory
Down the passage which we did not take
Towards the door we never opened . . .
T.S. ELIOT, *Four Quartets*

ONE

Two meaningful things enabled him to enjoy a calm, peaceful interlude in an otherwise hectic life. The first, a private log cabin in the woods. The second, collected poetic treasures in albums. The significance of each was never lost in the total picture of his being.

He retreated to the cabin every weekend that he could. Now, as he sat in the rocking chair on the porch, the serenity of the surrounding environment soothed away the residual agitation and anxiety that the demands of his job entailed. Here, he was able to relax and regroup his wits and sanity. No other place offered him that kind of solace.

On this Saturday early in July, the shade from the surrounding massive trees as well as a gentle breeze chased away the summer's oppressive heat. He could sit there for hours, and he often did, watching the wildlife parade before him. Deer would amble close to the cabin, smelling and tasting the vegetation along the way. They seemed to know over the nine years that he had been coming here that he was a friend and not a hunter. In the summer there was enough for the growing herd to eat, but in the winter he spread corn and apples out for them to feast on. He particularly worried about the little ones, some appearing far too frail to withstand the rigors of the barren woods. He would shudder on his long walks through the woods on even the coldest of days, knowing that they were cold blooded in the winter and that their winter coats were impervious. There was a little gully near by that they habitually bedded down in, at least sheltered from the wind. The birds would make lengthy visits to the many feeders set out for their enjoyment, interrupted occasionally by an aggressive squirrel trying to get to the sun seeds. Chipmunks and rabbits would scamper around in play or to forage, and an occasional wild turkey would plod along as if on an important mission. A resident red fox proudly trotted by on occasion as if claiming a form of ownership over the woods. As a lover of nature and an appreciator of its bounty, he often thought he should have become a forest ranger instead of an attorney.

Because a shingle roof would be prone to mildew in the deep woods, the cabin had a tin roof. That was a particular delight when it rained. The sound of the rain hitting the metal emphasized each drop's participation in a grand symphony. While at times thunderously loud, there was something soothing about the repetitive strikes. For the same reason, he had become enamored with chiming clocks, and the cabin and his apartment in the city contained an assortment of antique mantle and shelf clocks.

The imposing stone fireplace within the small confines of the interior made it possible for him to visit in the winter when his jeep could make it through. A few times he had been snowed in, and those had been marvelous times. He always had his laptop with him, so he could not escape the work input, but somehow the enchantment of the special containment more than offset the toil. Snow in the woods is nothing like the snow of the city. An enthralling beauty to behold. A crisp and clean cloak accentuating nature's smallest details, while at the same time creating an entirely different broad vista for tired, wondering eyes.

Eleven years ago, when he graduated from law school and had passed the New York State Bar Exam, he had a number of options. Several law firms were interested in him. A couple of corporate legal departments had put out feelers to him. A trade association aggressively repeated an offer of employment. Then, an opportunity arose to work for the United States Congress. The Staff Director of the Senate Foreign Relations Committee called him on the recommendation of one of his professors, and even without an in-person interview offered him a senior position on the staff. Being young and unattached, the prospect seemed quite interesting, and the idea of moving to Washington excited him. He would give it a year, and if it did not work out he would then return to New York City. If nothing else, the stint would be quite impressive on his resume.

Ten years had passed, and he was still there. There were continuing great pressures and demands from the work of the Committee and its activist Members, and the hours were long. Many a time he worked until the early hours of the morning. The challenges were varied and engrossing, and he often found himself involved with legal issues involving foreign relations that were novel and significant. A supporting role, with behind-the-scene machinations suited his temperament and style. International law represented a fascinating intellectual endeavor, and he relished employing a growing expertise in the subject. Adding to the strain, he had spent three years going to law school in the evenings to gain a Masters of Law in Public International and Comparative Law. A most respected addition to his credentials.

Sensing that he needed a special place to offset the repeated turmoil, as soon as he had decided he would stay in Washington, he found this wonderful cabin in the hills of West Virginia. After a two-hour drive, he was in another world. It had turned out to be one of the best decisions he had ever made.

Now, all of this was going to change.....drastically. There would be no more Capitol Hill involvement and intrigue. The cabin, at least this cabin, would soon belong to another fortunate person. It took only three weeks to sell, and the closing was scheduled in four weeks.

He reached into his shirt pocket, and pulled out the letter that beckoned him to new horizons. He reread it again, knowing full well that for better or worse his life was about to change.

Dear Mr. Weyland: On behalf of the Trustees of Blantyre University, it gave me great pleasure to have extended an offer to you to join our distinguished faculty for the forthcoming school year, commencing the last week in August. We are most delighted that you have agreed to accept that offer. You will be part of the Political Science Department, and will teach two courses. An Introduction to International Law, is an undergraduate course. Advanced International Law, is a graduate course.

Blantyre University is one of the oldest institutions of higher learning in New Hampshire. Its rolling campus covers over a thousand acres, and there are 43 buildings that serve our enlightened academic community. The most modern equipment and technological achievements, unsurpassed by any other University in the nation, are found throughout the learning centers, and are readily available to faculty and students. Our faculty is comprised of many of the leading scholars in their fields, and is the envy of other colleges. Since our admission standards are so high, our student body is exceptional. You will find a warm welcome here, as well as a stimulating and challenging learning environment in a quaint and relaxed setting.

We have been most impressed by your credentials and experience, not to mention the glowing recommendations received by a number of our govern-

ment leaders. You will fit right in with our eminent collection of teachers, each dedicated to accomplishing the utmost for the students and the University.

Please report to Dr. Walker Cloverdale, Chairman of the Political Science Department, Room 623, Henderson Hall, no later than August 16th for briefings and other preliminary matters. Housing for faculty can be arranged for you by Janet Grier, Special Assistant for Housing, Rm 112, Cooper Hall.

If there are any other special needs that arise, members of my staff will be most happy to assist you. Once again, welcome aboard!

Sincerely,

Weston Bridgewater, Chancellor

It certainly was going to be difficult to give up the cabin. It had been his sanctuary. A tranquil pool within a tempest. He was determined to enjoy the short remaining time he had within the hospitable setting. Since he sold it furnished, he had only to pack up an assortment of books, clocks and other personal items. Knowing what such a place can do for him, he was fully resolved to find a similar haven if and when needed wherever he might be ensconced. Some symbols travel well.

Without a doubt, his most cherished possession was the three photo albums that accompanied him back and forth between the cabin and the city apartment. Not filled with pictures, beneath each plastic sleeve was a hand written poem that his father had given to his mother over the course of thirty-five years of courtship and marriage.

While working on Capitol Hill, he had associated with or had come in contact with many power movers of both the United States and other nations. To most observers, such persons would amply fall with the ambit of a description of "great men".

> *Lives of great men all remind us*
> *We can make our lives sublime,*
> *And departing, leave behind us*
> *Footprints in the sands of time.*
> HENRY W. LONGFELLOW

> *Be not afraid of greatness; some are born*
> *great, some achieve greatness, and some have*
> *greatness thrust upon them.*
> WILLIAM SHAKESPEARE

There are certainly great men in the context of history, and their lives and accomplishments have affected or been revered by many. Yet, there is a different kind of great man. A person who is unknown and whose name and feats go unrecorded in the annals of civilization. Such a person, however, has had a significant and lasting influence on a small group of persons, perhaps even only a single individual. Just such a great man was his own father. Gilbert Weyland was a tower of intelligence, feeling, and perception. A kind, gentle and loving man. A firm believer in peace, justice and mercy. A man who had an unquenchable thirst for knowledge, translated into a homespun wisdom that served as a guiding light to his son whenever a dark interlude threatened his well being.

Raised in an extremely loving home had given Brandon Weyland good role models. Self-confidence arose in his consistent treatment by his parents as a human being, entitling him to be a part of family discussions and decisions. Not only was he loved, a feeling that he could wear as a cloak to ward off the vagaries of existence, but his parents worshipped each other. His mother, Theresa Weyland, had nursed his father through two prolonged, life-threatening medical conditions, and his father poured out his heart and soul to her in the poems not merely out of gratitude for those unselfish gestures of her love for him, but also for the support and understanding that served as a bedrock for the family. As an added expression of his love for her, on each of their wedding anniversaries and her birthdays, and at times not prompted by such a special occasion, a poetic offering would be forthcoming. Kept by her in a series of boxes, upon her death eight years ago and his father's passing five years ago, there was little in the estate except for these boxes and his father's library. Both were now a vital part of his personal domain. He had taken each poem and put it in the proper chronological order when such was discernible, and then encased each in the albums to preserve them in a way that he could read and appreciate them. He did this often and with a never-ending admiration for the depth of sensitivity and devotion of the poet. As his son, those sentiments translated into a living creed.

Since the albums were with him on all of his sojourns, they were constantly available to soothe and inspire him. A favorite endeavor was to randomly flip to a page, and to reread one of the gems and to feel the warmth spread through his own spirit. An old friend. Tried and true. Comfortable and constant.

One of the albums even now rested so naturally on his lap. He righted it, opened it and turned over a number of pages. His eyes rested on the words before him as a discerning lover of nature would gaze out upon a meadow with colorful wild flowers.

> *15th Anniversary —*
> *This is a moment for realization*
> *That dreams, from glittering worlds above,*
> *Acquire a living, vital translation,*
> *And a firmer habitation, in a life of love.*
> *All calendars and seasons without end*
> *Humbly wait upon realities that spilled*
> *The perfume of each moment, and set them free,*
> *To add to hearts already filled*
> *With throbbing memories unto eternity.*
> *Your Gilbert*

> *18th Anniversary —*
> *Is it possible that from the day we wed*
> *I've left a single thing unsaid*
> *That to a tender comrade and dearest wife,*
> *Traveling with me through a joyful life,*
> *Would still sound as sweet, though repetitive,*
> *And fall upon ears eagerly waiting and receptive?*

> *While feeling the noblest and doing the best,*
> *The passage of time by the clock is no test —*
> *In living deeds and in thoughts, sometimes unsaid,*
> *We measure time in heart throbs instead.*
> *Your Gilbert*

At least the poems would go with him to Blantyre. He would have them to find refuge in the words and meanings if such were needed. Always the optimist, he had a feeling that the poems alone would be enough to see him through this adventure. At this point, he did not want to look any further down the road. He did not believe that an individual has a destiny that is beyond comprehension and control. Each building block of his experience, expertise, and character, would present him with the choices for his life structure. He was more curious about what it might be than concerned about when it might be.

TWO

Not very far away, another soul contemplated an impending teaching job at Blantyre University. Lucy Post, who had just turned twenty-four, was by most criteria far too young to be a professor. Yet, she was also considered of too tender years at nineteen to have graduated college, and at twenty-two to have garnered both a master's and a doctorate in Environmental Science. Unrestrained by an educational system, and personally undaunted in utilizing her intellectual abilities, she catapulted herself beyond normal expectations and ordinary learning. All due in large part, she was sure, because her parents were exceptional people.

It was ironic that she should wind up teaching at Blantrye University. Her parents, Justin and Estelle Post, were legends at the school. They were fond of telling Lucy that legends are not the product of the actual events, but are made up in the telling and retelling of what people thought was happening at the time. The two are often far apart.

What Lucy did know, as the result of repeated questions to them, was that her father had been a professor and her mother a senior in 1974, the year of the great uprising by the students at Blantyre. She encouraged them to talk about those times as much as possible, and she never tired of hearing their love story. Amidst the turmoil and despair, they had fallen in love. They had left during the school year, married, and two years later Lucy was born in the same small house in which they had always lived. The details of what drove them to leave, and their involvement in what had transpired, were not favorite topics of conversation, so she had to piece together what had been said at various times together with what she had read about what later became known as the Post Rebellion. Her father had apparently been the accused instigator of the student upheaval, and her mother had been his staunchest student ally. Wonderful fodder for her romantic mind to dwell upon, and to add to the aura of noble causes and leadership qualities of her flesh and blood.

Justin Post had been an author. He had published two rather famous books. The second one had been published some six months before Lucy's birth. He never wrote another book. It was her mother who rose to fame through her activist role in all sorts of environmental and civil rights causes. In the process, she had authored numerous popular and influential articles and books. When she became the President of AGE, the Alliance for a Green Earth, fifteen years ago, her speaking engagements were booked up more than a year in advance. Justin was the silent partner and speech-polisher, ever prodding Estelle, inspiring her on to ever more creative ideas and actions. Together they faced all foes and adversities, each supporting the other and adding strength and character to new and on-going ventures.

Whenever her mother traveled while Lucy was still young, at times seemingly to the far ends of the planet, her father stayed behind to serve as both mother and father. In that invigorating and nurturing setting, Lucy thrived. When she was old enough, they all traveled together. The entire world was hers to discover, and her navigators were always close by with a precise scientific explanation that was elucidating and fascinating. With that sort of parental involvement, environmental science loomed as a natural calling.

Her mother's soft voice and gentle, guiding hand led her to master life's upheavals. The growing years were not measured in terms of obstacles but in challenges. Lectures were couched in such rational, placid terms, Lucy learned without strain or confusion. Her father's humor tinged so many of the daily rituals of living that she often had a smile on her lips. What she recalled more than anything else were the proverbs that her father cast out without hesitation or invitation. Especially when they were not relevant at all, she laughed the hardest.

Her mother's books filled her with the wonderment of the accomplishments attached to dedication to a cause. A care and concern for the world and its components and people filled the pages and were absorbed in her mind and heart. Her father's two books, which she had read so many times that she had lost count, balanced her growing worldly outlook with the specter of an individual pursuit of happiness and understanding. Other books, devoured en route, had assisted in bringing her to this early maturation and eagerness to embrace responsibility. She felt grown up. An adult in mind and spirit. Ready to take on the world. Primed to climb to a position of leadership. With such powerful parental support, the time was right for her to become her own beacon of light to pierce the darkness of ignorance and apathy.

With the relative ease of reaching this juncture, some aspects of her life had rushed by. She regretted not having a real close female friend. There had also been no lasting male friend to share the extensive affection she could impart. Observing and sensing the great love between her mother and father, she felt she had much to give. She was not impatient, but was ready to share with a special person the essence of her being. It would come, just as her parents had found each other and gone on to claim the richness of their love.

This sunroom was her father's favorite room. She knew why. The view was marvelous, and she never tired of it either. The flow of the river, the majestic hillsides, and the uninterrupted foliage on the steep terrain where no building was possible, filled an observer with a sense of enthrallment and awe. A similar feeling she had when she gazed up at the stars, or the first time she saw the giant redwoods on a trip with her parents to the West Coast. While a new addition had been put on the house, and other parts renovated at various times, this room had remained intact.

As she stared out the tall picture windows at the familiar yet seemingly ever-changing sight, her mother entered the room.

"Ah, Lucy. I see you have inherited your father's extended ability to dream."

"I like to think of it as serene meditation. A process by which a half-baked idea becomes fully cooked."

"I sure am going to miss my little darling. Estelle put an arm around Lucy's shoulder and pressed it firmly with those steady fingers. "You have given us so much pleasure. I wish I had been able to have more children. I would have been deliriously happy."

"Dad would have had to double-up on his proverbs."

"I don't think that would be a problem for him, just for us. I often feel he has gotten to the point where he makes them up."

"The way he spouts them, who can take the time or has the energy to research their authenticity?"

"Are you all packed?"

"Yes. I have all of your books and Dad's two classics. What more do I need?"

"A toothbrush might come in handy."

"I am glad you mentioned that. I surely would have overlooked it. Too many details to deal with."

"I have prepared an itinerary for you. We'll be globe hopping for the next six weeks. Your father is busy polishing my speeches and lining up his recreation possibilities at the places we are invited to. But, we'll surely be back here at Thanksgiving and Christmas for all of us to be together. We've never missed those family times, and because of you, dear sweetie, they have special meaning for us."

"And for me as well." She hugged her mother, feeling, as always, safe and secure.

Estelle Post felt extremely blessed. Not only was Lucy the most delightful child a parent could have, but her Justin was constantly at her side to bolster any sagging weakness. A woman could not wish for more than a deep love from a wonderful man who was her husband and very best friend. Last year, when they had celebrated their twenty-fifth wedding anniversary, Justin had given her a charming silver locket. There was room inside for two pictures, one on each side. One was a blurry snapshot that a stranger had taken of them on the first picnic they had gone on at Blantyre. The second was a recent picture, with a picture of Lucy superimposed above their heads. Their love and their angel. An encased significant life, worn constantly around her neck. All she had to do was to touch it, and tears of joy filled her eyes and a warmth spread from her heart to all parts of her body.

"There you go crying, again. If you don't stop, I'll join you for sure."

Crying came easily to the two women. Happy or sad events brought this common trait to the fore. A reflection of the close affinity that the two shared. They were truly contemporaries rather than mother and daughter.

For Lucy, it was not difficult to remember the times, the many times that her mother supported her actions and activities. The right blend of logic and caution put impressions in perspective. In all of the years, she could not remember one instance in which her mother raised her voice or had said a harsh word to her. A very tough act to follow! Little wonder that her mother was her idol. More than anyone else she wanted to turn out just as she had. What greater tribute could a child give to a parent?

Justin Post entered the room. Before him he could gaze upon his beloved wife, Estelle. The years had been very kind to them. Capturing the second chance in his life at love had been the elixir of his happiness. Fortunate for him to learn the lesson from a soul searing time of indecision leading to debilitating inaction. His Estelle, once a floundering young woman had showed him with her deep devotion and steady design that a union founded on love can flourish. Great pride followed each of their accomplishments. He gladly fell back to foster her advancement, recognizing early on that she had a much more sustainable drive than he had. Through it all the loving relationship gave him great comfort. He gradually learned what Estelle had known from the beginning — such was fulfillment in itself.

Lucy was the bountiful fruit of this powerful union. Every effort at building her character was rewarded in an individual exuding warmth of sentiment and assertive confidence as needed. She galvanized the family bond, and reinforced the creed they lived by — the greatest joy is in the giving of love. The noblest of human adventures is to raise a child to become a sensitive and productive addition to society, instilling life so that the outer reaches of living can be captured and experienced.

Justin exclaimed robustly:

> *Just as it oughta,*
> *Mother and Daughter;*
> *Both a warm ray of sunshine,*
> *And I can boast that both are mine.*

Lucy, quick to respond in kind, "An Eskimo proverb, I suppose?"

"No. A Post original. But, if it's a proverb you are after, try to fathom this one — 'the daughter who rebukes her father's wisdom opts for an arduous course through life.'"

Lucy and Estelle laughed. Estelle chimed in, "That's an incubator proverb. He learned it in the nursery when you were born. I am very surprised he still remembers it, or even that they let him escape from the building."

Justin responded equally as jovial, "No fair. Two against one."

Lucy chimed in, "It takes two of us to show you your one weakness."

He approached, and hugged them both. From a point early in his life when he could only look backwards, he had succeeded in attaining the posture where he neither had to look back nor ahead. The most meaningful things in life were right before him at this moment. His agonizing, painful youth had been wonderfully offset by a placid and contented adulthood. His fascination for proverbs endured. Each could capsulize a moment or a feeling as nothing else could.

A contented mind is a continual feast
[ENGLAND].

THREE

The faculty garden apartment complex was at the edge of the campus, with most of the units facing thick woods. Brandon was able to get a top unit facing a clump of white pines, and he felt very relaxed instantly. A small balcony, a little reminiscent of the cabin's porch, enhanced a feeling of a connection with nature. As soon as the moving truck arrived, and he placed the furniture and set up the clocks, his comfort factor was complete. It would take longer to unpack the books, but that would be a labor of love. Certain possessions have a meaning that transcends the ordinary. So far, so good!

As he stood in front of Henderson Hall, he read the brass plaque to the left of the doors. *Erected in 1997. Dedicated to the memory of Kate Henderson, who died after twenty-four years as a beloved teacher at Blantyre University. Her tireless service and devotion to the University and the students that have passed through its portals are exemplary. This edifice stands as a lasting symbol of those significant accomplishments.*

Dr. Walker Cloverdale, the head of the Department, greeted him warmly with a broad smile. He was an elderly gentleman with a balding head and stooped shoulders. His voice resonated with composure and conviction, undoubtedly the natural result of years of teaching and the various presentations of scholarship findings. "Welcome to BU, Mr. Weyland."

Brandon settled into a seat before the wide, cluttered desk. The computer screen displayed a screen saver of rotating pictures of wildlife. A most pleasant scene to watch when his eyes wandered during the ensuing conversation.

Over the next two hours, Brandon learned more about the University and the Political Science Department than he knew he could remember. There were many strict rules and cautionary designs, and a repeated warning against the involvement or even appearance of personal involvement with a female student. A number of sexual harassment cases brought against the University had raised tight restrictions. Brandon could not help but conclude that with so many regulations, so many dangers and pitfalls to be wary of, there would seem to be little ambition or production of unguarded teaching. With cross purposes in mind, it was merely an invitation to stumble.

His next stop was at the Cornwell Library, a most impressive structure sitting at the epicenter of the campus. He had an appointment with Linda Whitman, the Head Librarian, for a tour of the facility.

Linda Whitman slouched down in her office chair, swiveled away from the desk. Gazing out of the window, and staring at nothing in particular, she was absorbed in a mental turmoil. Not particularly looking forward to another school year, with the ongoing struggles for resources and space, as well as a hostile divorce fresh in the making, she was feeling quite sorry for herself. Over a period of ten years, she had worked hard and steadily to become the head librarian, but not without a very high price. Her marriage had suffered, and her fervor had steadily diminished. Part of the reason she had worked long hours was that there was really nothing to go home to. Larry was a decent man, but he was too shallow for her intellectual and emotional drive. Their physical union was unsatisfying, and there were many regrets for marrying him. She had been young and inexperienced with men, and he seemed to be the person she thought she wanted. She was glad that they had no children. That complexity in her life would have added a greater difficulty in making choices.

It was not every day that such an attractive man came through her door. When she swiveled her chair around at the sound of the knock, she was taken by surprise by the male specimen standing in the doorway.

"Mrs. Whitman, I am Brandon Weyland. I believe you are to guide me through this magnificent abode of knowledge."

Gazing on the fine face and the broad smile, sensing the strength and confidence carried in his stature, she secretly caught her breath. "Yes, I have been expecting you," she responded in her most pleasant voice, adding to herself, "but not expecting what I see."

Linda rose from the chair and clasped his outstretched warm hand firmly. The mere touch sent a shiver of pleasure up her spine. She had been without the close contact of a man for far too long. "Let me show you around, and please interrupt me if you have any questions.....or comments."

For him, it surely was a meeting of some significance. He had been associated with so many female workers on the Hill, females seeking far more than just day-to-day administrative functions, not to pick up on the nuances of the woman's gaze and the inflections in her voice. He guessed her to be in her early 30s, and she had taken good care of herself. The brown hair was neatly piled in a bun on her head, and the figure was ample in the form-fitting suit that encased it. Not a typical image of a librarian, if such a thing existed anymore.

The tour lasted two hours, and by its end he was able to conclude that this was a first-rate library. Linda was an exceptional librarian, and her mastery of the collections reflected a vast intellect and a deep commitment to her work. He also picked up on the free conversation that she was divorced and living alone in a house a few miles from the University. An invitation of sorts to an opportunity that most males would relish and unhesitatingly take advantage of. It would be one item to store in his memory for easy recollection. Yet, he had side-stepped many such temptations before. A relationship had to be special to be meaningful. Somehow, at this point he did not want to start down this new road with any initial encumbrances. Vistas needed to be broad, sensations unrestricted. So, after a polite parting, he headed on his way. There was no way she could hide the disappointment in her voice, and once again the touch of his hand sparked an emotion too long dormant.

Back in his apartment, he grabbed an album and headed for the balcony. It was instantly pleasurable just to sit, and he made a mental note to buy a rocking chair as soon as convenient. Staring out into the trees, he tried to recall the details of his visit with Dr. Cloverdale. They seemed a jumble of cautionary rules, and there was no doubt that he would have to learn the intricacies as he went along.

He made a quick trip to the kitchen for his staple food — a peanut butter and jelly sandwich with slices of cucumber immersed in the jelly. He was about to take the first bite when he looked down at what appeared to be a bike path through the woods. A young woman was on it, jogging towards the building. Most likely a student, as she looked quite young. There was something very fetching about her. The gray sweat suit could not hide the trim shape. Sunlight filtered through the trees, adding an aura of mystery as she glided so gracefully along the path and through the shadows. With some surprise, she waved up at him. He waved back, a smile crossing both of their mouths in unison.

As Lucy jogged along the trail, she had looked up to see a young man at his balcony railing. It was the apartment directly above hers. He must also be a faculty member, and in her usual unabashed manner, she waved at him. His reciprocal act had brought that quick, easy smile to her face. For a happy person, a smile is a mantle of flowers, perpetually fresh, always a gesture of welcome. One of the multitudes of proverbs and sayings that her father had spouted over the years flashed through her mind. *The grand essentials of happiness are: something to do, something to love, and something to hope for.* [Allan K. Chalmers]

In the waning light of the day, he opened the album. The pages represented more than just memories immortalized in the poems, they were a reminder that each person can and should learn individualized guide marks along the road of life. A reassurance to the traveler that meaningful progress can be had as well as a beckoning symbol to those who follow later that the road is passable. For all, a destination of opportunity, solutions, and hope is attainable.

13TH ANNIVERSARY

If I were asked why I loved you so
When I saw you first those years ago,
And I knew what good fortune came my way
To enthrall the soul — so that even now I say
That every fibre in me felt it true —
There's nothing real in this world but you.

It's been with a mounting sense of pride
That I've always had you by my side,
Smiling bravely behind a hidden pain,
Suffering worry without complain —
A pillar of strength — guiding, inspiring
Satisfaction and fulfillment beyond desiring.

Since the day in a love compact we did enter
You've been the pulsating, gravitational center;
Like a magnet that bits of metal does attract,
You've always drawn me to you as a happiness contact;

And to the extent these contacts do increase,
I hope to crown your days with wondrous peace.
                                                  Your Gilbert

7TH ANNIVERSARY

As the tides of life ebb and flow,
     The links in our chain of kinship
Hold fast and strong, and even grow
     At a subtle but inexorable clip;
Loving you with a profound continuity
     Is the privilege, I joyously realized
O'er these years of unbroken unity,
     That is to be sustained and emphasized;

And though the shadows that sometimes flit
     Across the store of uncounted bliss
Leave some traces, they do not mar a bit
     The constancy of a love like this;

While after each joy we must feel some pain
     Newly tempered, bittersweet but sublime,
Fulfillment is yet to be — a total gain —
     As our love is an Oasis in Time!
                                                  Your Gilbert

Closing the album slowly, he pressed his palm on the cover. This was the rich family history that let him gain often needed perspective. Life's greatest significance is to find, to hold on to, and to worship love.

FOUR

As he always did, Justin grasped Estelle's hand as the airplane took off. Even with the numerous flights to all parts of the world, she was still uneasy on the takeoffs. His steady hand was here for this, as with so many other things. A loving spouse and a loving daughter filled her treasure chest with life's purest delights. To enhance the beneficence, she had an opportunity to fight for a cause in which she deeply believed. The influences that had given her direction were easily bestowed on others. Being a leader was not part of her grand design. It just happened, and there were times she wondered whether her early association with Ted Amherst had imbued her with an imposing role model. Not only had he been her boyfriend before Justin, he had been the leader of the students. His charisma and mannerisms easily brought the students to hang on his words and to follow each and every direction offered in his pronouncements. She had forcefully disagreed with him in those closing days, and her words were the sole contrary utterances that were carried off in the current of Ted's monologues.

Staring out the small window at the specks of farm land passing below, Estelle turned her thoughts back to those college days, back to a time when her life was in turmoil from competing passions. If Justin had not entered her life, bringing a form of reason and stability, there was no way of knowing where should would have wound up. One event, one person can alter a life's course. She liked to think that she had all of the basic ingredients to command a worthwhile life, but it took the presence of Justin in her life to enable her to bring them out in proper order — to make sense out of the jumble of thoughts and feelings that had plagued her. If her life ended today, it would have to be described as full and meaningful. How many others had such a feeling of satisfaction and accomplishment?

Coincidentally, Justin's thoughts had carried him back to the past. His eyes were closed. The droning of the jet's engines acted as a thrust to further transport his mind to an earlier period. Usually, he did not like to take a concentrated look into the past. The early segments contained little of what he could take pride in. One special frustration had grown over the years. He deeply regretted not finishing his teaching term at Blantyre. Numerous notes had been prepared for the seminar sessions that were left undelivered. He was sure that if given enough time he could have given the students a firmer and more positive direction. After all, he had turned the most ardent critic and activist around completely. Ted Amherst, despite his involvement in the troubles that ensued, had awakened to a societal sense of purpose. Justin had never thrown those seminar notes away. Every so often he would look through them, and imagine how he would have used them in his grand strategy to turn the radicalism focused on the university inward to resolve the individual root problems which had so much to do with the frustration with the system. Given enough time, he could have made a difference. It was not to be. Yet, that gnawing feeling stayed with him, haunting his spirit each time the thought arose.

Even as Justin reflected upon his own role in the 1960s and the production of his first book, *The Disestablishmentarians,* which had graphically depicted that extraordinary time period and its surrounding events and personalities, it was a later book by another author that helped capture its essence. It matched his own retrospective view. Richard N. Goodwin, in his 1988 book, *Remembering America,* astutely observed:

[T]o remind that men and women can live as if their world was malleable to their grasp; and that, true or false, to live in this belief is to be the most authentically alive.

Justin, closing his eyes and transporting himself back in time, to stand before those young people, in what would have been the next seminar session on anarchism. His design was to emphasize that coordinated, collective thought and action could do much to change social, political, and economic ills. The emphasis was to be on the mental force of will without the distractions and misinterpretations inherent in overt force, particularly if resulting in physical destruction. Such a theme of thought may not have stemmed the rebellious aftermath, but it may have given some additional thought, some mental impact that may have lessened the forceful alternative. Perhaps, it may have swayed some not to participate, thereby negating some of the overall destruction. That he would never know, but it certainly would have made him feel better to have tried to turn the head of the wild beast.

Justin would have begun his remarks by quoting from a portion of the Day of Affirmation Address given by Robert F. Kennedy at the University of Capetown, Capetown, South Africa, on June 6, 1966.

> *"There is," said an Italian philosopher, "nothing more difficult to take in hand, more perilous to conduct, or more uncertain in its success than to take the lead in the introduction of a new order of things." The road is strewn with many dangers. First is the danger of futility; the belief there is nothing one man or woman can do against the enormous array of the world's ills ...*
>
> *Yet ... each time a man stands up for an ideal, or acts to improve the lot of others, or strikes out against injustice, he sends a tiny ripple of hope, and crossing each other from a million different centers of energy and daring, those ripples build a current that can sweep down the mightiest walls of oppression and injustice.*

That would have been followed by a forceful dictate in the 1960 Founding Statement of the SNCC, the Student Non-Violent Co-Ordinating Committee,

> *We affirm the philosophical or religious ideal of nonviolence as the foundation of our purpose, the presupposition of our belief, and the manner of our action.*
>
> *Nonviolence, as it grows from the Judeo-Christian tradition, seeks a social order of justice permeated by love. Integration of human endeavor represents the crucial first step towards such a society.*
>
> *Through nonviolence, courage displaces fear. Love transcends hate. Acceptance dissipates prejudice; hope ends despair. Faith reconciles doubt. Peace dominates war. Mutual regards cancel enmity. Justice for all overthrows*

injustice. The redemptive community supersedes immoral social systems.

By appealing to conscience and studying on the moral nature of human existence, nonviolence nurtures the atmosphere in which reconciliation and justice become actual possibilities.

Then would have come his own synopsis of those tenuous times they were living through. Even if society was deemed to be out of control, remedies should not replicate a similarly unconfined, unstructured response. The greatest potential to affect coveted change had to be through a unified movement to educate and set by example that productive alternatives were available to society. Civil disobedience held the promise to be the most effective means to such an end. Electing those who believed in such a course, at both the national and local levels, was a necessary step. Ingrained in law, a progressive movement would be the ripples through society that Robert F. Kennedy had described as possible. Righting political disillusionment would lead to permanent changes.

The closing segment of his lecture would have involved the other important aspect that he believed so firmly in. The concept that the students needed to hear and to think about. It was exactly the same theme that he would later elaborate on in his second book. Besides the desirability of collective civil disobedience, there is an inner demand and purpose that each individual must heed. The potential for self-development, self-fulfillment. If this meant a splinter from group action and sentiment, then one must step away. The reason we are individuals, with unique identifiable features, is that there is some inner goal that needs to be focused on and given due attention. It may run counter to the main stream of thought and acceptability. It may, in an ironic fashion, be as radical in its separate components as the imprimatur affixed to the student rebellion. It might be as calm and as soothing as standing on a mountain top gazing out for fifty miles in every direction and watching the lush setting of a cultivated valley below. The human potential — infinite and indefatigable. As one satisfies hunger with food, the inner need for reaching as far as possible in the spectrum of the soul to experience the contentment and pride of doing the best that one can. To reach the outer limits of one's capabilities. To satisfy the civilized beliefs of accomplishing deeds to better the world around us. To read and act out the story within ourselves.

The never-to-be-held seminar was not the only regret that came to the fore. Pushed back to the deep recesses of his memory was his hurtful treatment, his inane involvement in losing his first love. His years with Estelle had been truly wonderful, and there was no reason for him to reach back so far into the past and punish himself for deeds that could not be undone or fully explained. For several years, however, the climactic episode crept further and further to his fully conscious moments. The details had long since lost their clarity, but the principle emerged as a disease beckoning for a cure. Once the idea took a stranglehold in his mind, the compulsion to effectuate it prompted the decision for action. Now, he would not be able to rest until he saw it through to completion.

Last night, as they were packing for the trip, Justin announced his idea to Estelle. "I am going to write a novel."

As anticipated, her reaction was one of encouragement. She had often urged him to write again. "Such talent is wasted in bolstering my endeavors," was her typical outpouring. Now that Lucy was away and they were on their own, Estelle agreed that such an intellectual involvement would be good for him. She had on numerous occasions tried to persuade him to go back to teaching. He had shown such great potential at Blantyre. Students needed the sort of inspiration and guiding hand that he was adept at giving.

"What will it be about?" She asked without breaking away from the packing.

"It will be a tale echoing the themes of my early books. A fictionalized account of the dilemma and mystery of youth."

Estelle turned to him and smiled. Returning to the packing, she thought no further on it. Justin watched her actions closely, knowing full well that the question would arise again as he became immersed in the writing.

The plane leveled off. Estelle pulled out her notes and started to mull over the forthcoming speech, her next seemingly unending involvement in a series of defenses of the future of the planet and the animal and plant species upon which the fragile ecology rested. Glancing over at Justin, his eyes were still closed. He overdid the trip preparations, as always, she thought to herself. No wonder he was so tired.

He was not sleeping. In fact, his mind was in overdrive. Now that he had decided to work on a novel, the various elements of the story languished in his mind. Somehow, he always knew that it was a story he had to write. Not to finally rid himself of any guilt, but as a sort of a tribute to folly and the enduring possibilities of making up for mistakes. The story would be larger than the story of Justin and Rosalind. It would be the story of young love, the passion diminishing any possibility for securing its future benefits. It would be the capturing, in a unique way, what might have been. A finding of a lost love. The closing of the circle.

It was to be the story of Donald Hurst, a middle-aged man who had a successful job, a kind and caring wife, and two teen-aged daughters who were well adjusted and good students. He had, however, one great guilt. He had squandered the first love that he had experienced with a very special woman while they were in college, Myra Hoffman. He had surrendered it because he had failed to recognize its true existence and potential. To quell the guilt and as a token to make up for that great mistake, he decided to write a novel about that love just for her. If he could find her, she would be the only one to ever read it. To solicit her understanding and forgiveness. To find that very special love anew.

Justin knew all too well that the real motive in this writing was to fully expose that regret and to once and for all lay it to rest. Surely, it is not productive to measure one's life in terms of regrets. That, however, is often easier said than done. Certain regrets loom quite large when others are affected by the deeds or non-deeds, as the case may be. Besides the lost chance to finish the seminar, the other major regret in Justin's life was the inability to recognize and seek the fulfillment of that first love. A failure of his own. Minute items in terms of the larger accomplishments of finding, holding, and satisfying the needs of a second love, as well as having a daughter of such depth and vitality. Yet, like a steady drip of water from a faucet, his whole being appeared to be gradually eroding beneath the incessant disturbing thoughts of these two items of his past. It could not be rationalized away.

Perhaps, by becoming the character in the novel, he could right that regret. His writer's imagination had long taken him beyond what might have been the actual facts of that love and the real essence of the woman. He knew that. The intervening years, the conjuring of events, real or imagined, revisiting of the whys and wherefores, left little doubt that he was no longer able to see it the way it probably had been. The saving grace was that he was still basically a writer, and even if he wandered from the truth and actuality, the plot outline otherwise provided a rather captivating story. Perhaps, even a tribute to all lost loves. He was now the character in the book, as well as the story teller. Would either or both emerge intact? Which one is the real one? Does it even matter?

Justin pulled out his laptop. Glancing over at Estelle, bent over the papers before her, he began his task. The story began to unfold on the lines before him. Fiction based on fact or fact based on fiction, it mattered not. The lessons were the same. The same taunting curiosity. If he wrote the story, or actually lived it, the essence would probably be the same. The writer's urge was as strong at this moment than it had been at any point in his life. The story was going to find its own way.

MEMORY HAVEN

It mattered little that he had to self-publish the novel. It had not been written as a potential source of income, or to garner success or recognition. It had been written for only one purpose. Only one set of eyes were destined to take in the words. Only one heart was to be softened by the thoughts conveyed. Only one person would be able to recognize its truth, its honesty. Only one individual was out there to forgive him.

He reread the book one more time. An absorbing story of the machinations of young love. Spirit and passion without consistency, without direction. A boy, seeking to be a man. A boy unable to understand who he was. A boy incapable of seeing that the girl was his quest. A girl, knowing only what she felt, powerless to convey its stability to the boy, and surrounded by the demands of parents, school and society. Both too torn to see the simple solution within their grasp. He, succumbing to the complexity, broke the fragile thread binding them together. The loss eventually leading to self-discovery. A heavy heart to calculate the void. Leaving only a guilty mind seeking release from the bondage of torment.

Numerous flashbacks. Amorous delights, body and mind. Dialogue exploring the curiosities, the apprehensions, the discoveries of the human entity searching for the niche for purpose and solace. The protagonists interacting between themselves and their surroundings. Young minds and young spirits, difficult to comprehend and manage struggles at various levels.

He closed the cover on the book, satisfied that he had captured the essence of what happened, and confident that she would see in it the same lesson. Here he was, a middle-aged man, with a wife and daughters, seeking what might have been in an earlier unsuccessful period of life. Certainly not maturity and responsibility at its best, yet overshadowed by a morbid curiosity to turn the hands of time backwards. To get a second chance and to have the opportunity to correct a major error in judgment. The confrontation of a great risk, possibly to jeopardize all he had, casting away all he was now. Too much of an unknown result between the two extremes — recovering what had been abandoned and the bolt of reality.

With the book laying in his lap, he reread the private detective's report. She had been located. A teacher in a middle school in New York City, she was living in Queens. She was divorced and had one child. The house address not far from the house she grew up in. The house that he had picked her up from so many times. The house, in which the basement gave them their first opportunity to explore their bodies and to quell the fire of young desires. The same basement that repeatedly offered them the opportunities to relish the meaning of those contacts beyond the mere physical results. Too many opportunities then squandered without need or justification.

He sat down to write the letter to be put in the book to be sent to her. He had composed it so many times in his head that his hand needed little concentrated guidance to carry out his will.

Dearest Myra –

This letter and this book may be unwelcome. Voices from the past can be from ghosts. They can torment you, or they can be warm, friendly reminders of happy times long ago. Many years have passed since you and I were a couple. Our relationship ended in an abrupt manner and with harsh overtones, all on my part. I am sure that this was hurtful to you, not to mention without reason or justification. In hind sight, all that contemptuous labeling was true. It has also been a great regret in my after years, days, and minutes. There is no rational excuse that I can offer for my behavior. I hurt you, and I destroyed a worthwhile relationship, cutting short the great promise that I now recognize it offered. It had been the sweetest romance of my life.

These feelings have prompted me to write the book that accompanies this letter. It is a fictionalized account of what I remember we were and what we had. Time may well have distorted some of the happenings, some of the reactions. You may well recognize some of the people, some of the places, some of the emotional sensations.

The book served two purposes for me. First, it forced me to recall what I had, and to face that it was destroyed at my own hand. Second, it has allowed me to vent my guilt, and in an unorthodox manner it is the extension of my apology to you.

It is a special book. Written only for you. No one else will ever read it. It is the most private of diaries, coupled with what a psychiatrist would have to hold in confidence if spilled out from the couch. I hope that you receive it in the spirit in which it is offered. Somehow I sense that you will understand my motive and intention.

That I have written it and sent it to you is all I dare do. You can keep me in the past, a painful memory to be ignored. Or, you can contact me. You can write to me at the address on the top of this letter or send me an email at the email address below it.

The book is my toast to the past. You can complete its transition to the present.

Don Hurst

Justin glanced over at Estelle. Such strong and determined features. There was no doubt that he was deeply in love with her, and had been since he had finally sorted out the facets of his life. So, why the compulsion to right a past mistake that should merely loom in the background as a learning experience? Was there a deeper meaning? Why was there a restlessness deep within him? Was there a basic discontent with himself? Or, was it really simpler than all of this? Did he require a personal involvement over which he had exclusive control? Was it Justin the writer supplanting Justin the husband and father? If the book came to fruition, what would be the next step? How many questions would he have to ask of himself to fully understand what was happening?

> *He who asks a question is a fool for five minutes; he who does not ask a question remains a fool forever.*
>
> [CHINA]

What if there are no answers? What if the endless chain of questions chokes him? What if the not knowing is attributable to not asking the simplest of questions with the most involved responses? When is enough? What is contentment? What is the meaning of life? Ironically, some of the same questions that he and Rosalind had attempted on numerous occasions to find answers to.

FIVE

Unaccustomed to a dilemma of this sort, she was not sure of the best way to handle it. When Justin told her about the novel he wanted to write, Estelle's initial reaction was to be supportive of his endeavor just as he supported her in each venture she undertook. On this trip, however, his entire demeanor had changed. He was a man driven to distraction. Consumed with the need to work on the novel. There was little time or energy for anything else. Instead of being by her side to share in her exploits, to bolster her every effort, and to ward off any barbs of opposition or criticism, he secreted himself in each hotel room they stayed in, working feverishly on this obsessive project. She was torn between saying something and offering a sympathetic ear if he cared to unload this omnipresent burden, or merely to give him space to work it all out on his own. To give him the opportunity to turn to her when and if he needed her. To let him know that she was there for him, and that such an offering took precedence over all of the other facets of her life. Such is not a dictate of love. It is the natural outpouring of the bond sealed with years of togetherness, both in flesh and spirit.

It also represented a rare chance for her to examine her own present and past life. An introspection that was delayed and cast aside with the daily involvement of job and family. The often overwhelming demands of being the head officer and prime advocate of an activist organization. Being a mother to what had to be one of the world's most inquisitive and intellectually demanding children. To fulfill and satisfy the love engendered to and by a warm, kind, understanding, and supportive man. There had been scarce time to put herself as the focal point of the grand scheme, placing all of the compartments in true perspective. At this moment, when for perhaps the first significant time that she could readily remember, she could look back at the days at Blantyre University with a blend of curiosity and sentimentality. Poignant memories.

> *Everybody needs his memories.*
> *They keep the wolf of insignificance from the door.*
> SAUL BELLOW

> *Every man's memory is his private literature.*
> ALDOUS HUXLEY

> *. . .[L]ittle threads that hold life's patches of meaning together.*
> MARK TWAIN

> *The hills of one's youth are all mountains.*
> MARI SANDOZ

> *The light of memory, or rather the light that memory lends to things, is the palest light of all. I am not quite sure whether I am dreaming or remembering, whether I have lived my life or dreamed it. Just as dreams do, memory makes me profoundly aware of the unreality, the evanescence of the world, a fleeting image in the moving water.*
> EUGENE IONESCO

Over the years, Estelle's parents had drifted apart, and their contact with her was minimal. Neither quite approved of her activist stance for causes they could not fully grasp. But, she was basically appreciative of the nurturing influence they had on her in the early years. In fact, she attributed a part of her resolve to the security and comfort the home had represented for her. There had been times that she had wished for a closer relationship with them so that Lucy could know a grandparent's love and involvement, but it just was not meant to be.

Nobody ever heard from or about Dr. Mington, the man who had been her mentor at Blantyre, only to eradicate that positive stature by taking physical advantage of her. For all intents and purposes, he had vanished from the face of the earth. Rita Mington, Dr. Mington's daughter who had emerged from the troubled home and marriage of her parents to be a bright and caring individual, had been in close contact with them for a few years after their marriage, but she had joined the Peace Corps and had died from Malaria in the Congo. Justin often displayed a great remorse at the loss of such a promising life. Estelle had gotten to the point of recognizing in her the potential that Justin had keenly observed. Rita had a keen sense of perception, and a piercing intellect that demanded constant vigilance just to keep up with her. When she and Justin engaged in dialogue, Estelle often was lost as to the innuendoes and subtleties of their procrastination.

For a number of years, Estelle had followed the exploits of Ted Amherst. He had taught in high school for several years, and then a seething restlessness apparently led him to a series of business-related jobs. The agitated spirit, so omnipresent in college, evidently did not allow him to settle down or to gain satisfaction from things at hand. Perhaps the need for the aura of leadership was a handicap he could not overcome. Not hearing anything about him for years now, she wondered if he had met a special woman and had married. Looking back, there was a mixed emotion for her as to his part in her life. The relationship had been shallow, but had filled a temporary void in her life. It had come at a time when she needed something to clutch to. A woman never forgets the first man she had sex with.

That evening, the opportunity arose for her to bring the present situation to the forefront. Justin seemed morose, and was not working on his book. She suggested that they go out for dinner, and he accepted readily. At dinner they talked about many things, particularly about the news-filled emails from Lucy describing her every action, her every thought. Yet, she sensed something was missing. He was responsive, but there was a noticeable dullness in his voice and an evident strain in his mannerism.

Back in the hotel room, any restraint she was capable of dissipated as a puff of smoke. "This suite is fancier than my tastes are comfortable with."

His response was slow, measured by the mood she had detected. "An important person should raise her comfort level accordingly."

Her voice was shaky, knowing full well that she might be opening a door that might best have been left closed. "Would it be appropriate for me to ask you a question?"

"Sure. But don't necessarily expect an appropriate answer."

"You already know what I am about to ask you, don't you?"

"Yes. I was merely wondering what took you so long."

"I suppose I thought you would talk to me about it when you were ready to share your agonizing with me. I can't hold back anymore. Your anguish is mine as well."

A tense moment of silence followed, as he looked deep into those devastating blue eyes, the eyes that had captured his attention and admiration from the beginning. As a boy might try to outguess a parent, he offered in a robust tone, "So, what is bothering me?"

"Yes. That is the way I would put it. I am, after all, unable to offer solutions without a problem to tackle."

"It's not a problem, as I see it."

"To me, anything that absorbs you so completely, to the point of total distraction, is a problem. Not since Blantyre have I seen you like this. Therefore, to me it is a monumental problem."

"You might be very disappointed to know that there is no major upheaval, no divergent behavior to contend with. The simple truth of it all is that I feel an uneasy void since Lucy has gone from under our wings. What has rushed in to take its place is this desire to write again. It is a demon of sorts. The idea for a plot has become obsessive in nature, and it is leading me to demands in the writing that I am unaccustomed to. While I had a variety of pressures to handle when I wrote the first two books, I truly felt that I was the master of the writings. I was the guiding hand, the driving impulse. Nonfiction can be laden with difficulties, but the ideas are transferred into the writing in a reasonable, sensible sequence. Fiction writing is quite a different beast. I think I have come up with a good story, and it lingers in my mind, and I am constantly reliving it as it unfolds. If I did not feel it was worth telling, I would not feel so close to it."

"It's Rosalind emerging in your guilty conscience, isn't it?"

"Yes. That was the impulse I started with. From guilt, I am not so sure. Whatever, it is beyond a single person or even a series of events. The writer in me has totally replaced me as the person I was before I wrote that first word of the story. It is a story I feel I must write." He looked off into the distance, and Estelle had the disquieting sensation that he was visualizing something that she would never be able to see.

Grasping her hand, the motion was familiar and comforting. That hold and what it symbolized would not be jeopardized, but there was no way that he could adequately portray to her the compulsion driving this endeavor. He barely understood it himself.

Later, long after she had fallen asleep in his arms, he gently released her and returned to the writing. Seeking release from the torment bridging a tale from a writer's mind to the paper for others to share. He reread an earlier portion to bring the characters to full life.

The empty screen greeted his daily ritual to retrieve email messages. In the rush of events and his expectations stretching beyond normal limits, he was beginning to feel that he had miscalculated the results. Disappointment grew. The battle for the saving of his soul boarded on defeat.
Finally, after three weeks, to his elation a message arrived.

Don: I was absolutely floored by your contact and the flattering story you have written about me. Is it really me? Or, what you thought I was? I loved it. You are a wonderful writer, and I hung on every word, every idea.

Your guilt really shows itself. But, I think you are harder on yourself than you deserve. You really shouldn't blame yourself so completely. We were both young. Yes, I was hurt at the time, but that hurt did not linger with me. You were my first boyfriend. As such, you will always occupy a special place in my memory. I was infatuated with you long before you even noticed me. Our relationship had many positive aspects to it, and I feel it in some ways forced me to grow up.

Rather than you, I think the greatest damage to my confidence and sense of worth was done by my father. He ruled the house, was very stern, rarely showed any affection, and nothing I did ever pleased him. In spite of his political liberalism, he was anything but liberal with his family. My mother and I walked on egg shells. We were constantly on edge. To this day, that was the experience that has affected me the most.

I did a pretty good job messing up the rest of my life on my own. I suffered through a marriage to a man I did not love. The only good thing that came from it was a daughter whom I love dearly. I am a grandmother. She is married to a decent man, and I dote on my two grandchildren without reserve.

I have recently emerged from a long-term relationship that was, in hind sight, not completely satisfying. The one sustaining constant in my life has been my job. I have been a teacher for all of these years, and have never lost the excitement and challenge of working with young children. In that respect I am probably still a child myself, and glad of it! That sense of accomplishment has seen me through many a dark day.

I am finally starting to feel good about myself. It is almost as if I have found life anew. Perhaps I am just getting a glimmer of understanding of who I am in terms of living. Having been in therapy for many years, it is about time I made some progress! Above all, I am fortunate to have some good, close friends. They have helped me so much along the way. Some of these friends are people we knew together in college — Judy Wolfson, Brenda Stalls, Deena Guilder. Do you recall them? I have mentioned you and the book to them. Strangely, they do not remember you. Don't take that personally. It is not a slap in the face. After all, you were not to them as you were to me. They want to read the book, but I will not relinquish my copy or part with the dear sentiments that you inscribed inside the cover. Besides, I do not want to breach your pronouncement that no one else should read it.

Any other decision rests with you. You are a voice from my past, alright. Not an unwelcome one. Reading the book has already brought back a whole bunch of memories. I am sure as I reread it, and that I will, I will derive even more thoughts and pleasure from it.

Myra

Justin leaned back in the chair. Author and character reading and digesting the words. A debilitating creative process for the author, for the mind will take him to a life that only the character will live. What else would he have to give up in the process?

SIX

Much of Lucy's composure had been lost. Teaching was not as easy as she had anticipated. Mastery of the subject matter was not the smooth road to gaining and keeping the attention of students who were older than she. It was as if there was a natural resentment towards her that she could not seem to overcome. Even with all of the self-confidence she had when she had first entered the classroom, the spark had not come as she thought it would. It weighed heavily on her bearing. She was not the solid emotional fortress that she was in the inviting home environment. The weakening segments of her structure were crumbling before her eyes, and she even dreaded the next teaching class. A far cry from the excitement and boldness that preceded the first one.

The unanticipated reaction and results left her stunned and bewildered. It seemed irrational that she could not control this situation. Convinced that her ultimate goal was teaching, then why was it so difficult to accomplish? A door that locked automatically, clanging shut with such severity that the sound obliterated all of her thoughts of reason and perseverance. A door that might never be opened. A true captive of her own making.

She had never lied to her parents before, and she did not equate telling them that all was fine, when it was not, as an untruth. Dreading their disappointment in her that might match the disillusionment she had in herself, it seemed like an act of kindness not to disrupt their tranquil existence. After all, she had to focus on a reality of her own choosing. This was merely a temporary setback. Time and concentrated effort would salve the initial wounds of uncertainty and miscommunication. If it did not, then she was being introduced to a new dimension to her character, a weakness that she would not tolerate. All she need do would be to reinforce the basic ingredients of her being, remind herself of the person she knew she could be to accomplish the meaningful tasks that her destiny prescribed. Yet, she had not been prepared for this emotional scarring.

WITHER IS FLED THE VISIONARY GLEAM?
WHERE IS IT NOW, THE GLORY AND THE
DREAM?
W. WORDSWORTH

She knew that her parents would tell her that this was the character building stage of her life, and upheavals and obstacles produced a sturdier individual. Attested to by the confusion, this definitely was both an upheaval and an obstacle. Unaccustomed to failure, it was something she could not and would not readily accept. She would not listen to that small voice in the back of her mind advising her to leave and take a different path. The one thing that had become crystal clear was to do battle with herself first.

First resolve what must be done; solutions
will then become evident. [CHINA]

We must be willing to let go of the life we have
planned, so as to have the life that is waiting for us.
[E.M. FORSTER]

What lies behind us and what lies before us are tiny
matters compared to what lies within us.
[RALPH WALDO EMERSON]

Back in her apartment, emotionally exhausted, Lucy sprawled into an easy chair. Rented with the rest of the furniture, she had reserved this over-sized chair for reading. A fitful sleep was shortened by the strains of Shostakovich's 5th Symphony, music that she knew so well. The booming classic was, along with Mahler's 1st Symphony, her father's favorites. The melodic strains were coming from the apartment above, where the young man on the balcony had waved to her. She had not seen him in the two weeks since then, but the familiar music added just the right soothing gloss to her weak moment. She settled back in the chair, closed her eyes, and let the music obliterate the negative thoughts that had gripped her.

Brandon was also settling down deep into the chair he reserved for comfort and thought. While his early classes had been tiring, due mainly to the extensive preparation he had to put into them, the classes themselves had gone extremely well. The role of teacher proved to be highly stimulating. The students were attentive and responsive. Having practical experience in the subject matter proved helpful. Using real, current problems and relating them to the often dry subject principles led to interesting discussions and questions, and served to reemphasize those principles.

The impression he had gleaned was that young people can be classified as mind searchers. Boundless inquisitiveness is offset only by the struggle to fit the answers into the whole picture. It is very frustrating to get snippets of information and piece-meal guidance to put them together. Perhaps it is the preoccupation with the transitions, forcing guesswork to fill in the gaps, which make the process more difficult to hold and use. Even the majority of the students in his graduate course had little certainty where they fit into the larger scheme of society. He had to admit that such was not an easy quest.

The computer age has introduced the concept of instant gratification. A pervasive impatience has grown with projects that need excessive planning and implementation. A similar mode for ideas. Unless they are spelled out clearly, their implications readily apparent, they are often discarded for quicker, seemingly more gratifying results. He had been much the same way. When he had crossed the line, perhaps aptly delineated as the line of maturity, was difficult to pinpoint.

With this involvement in teaching, he confirmed what he had wrestled with when young. The trip to maturity need not be a continuing struggle. It need not be rushed. There may be only one distant destination, which may not be as important as the series of steps one reaches along the way. Some of these points can be planned; many merely are the products of the journey. The most important aspect is to recognize the junctures and to consider them *pondering points*. Places to rest, to regroup, and to dwell upon the fruits of the mental labor exerted to reach that resting place or crossroad. What does it mean for the moment? How can it best be employed to build on past pondering points? How can it ease and direct the steps to follow? A most important lesson to learn is that there is nothing shameful, or necessarily a sign of weakness or failure, in taking a step backwards. At times, that might be the best vantage point to see the future course of action in a clearer and more meaningful manner. Equally important, the reality that the long term goal may truly never be reached or even that is not actually necessary to be attained. A particular pondering point may turn out to be the most satisfying, the most fulfilling. If one, out of impatience or greed, skips or fails to adequately know or understand a pondering point, then that moment is lost both for its present value as well as the necessary bridge between past actions and the demanding future ones. The past experience is muddled and useless. The prophetic words of John Greenleaf Whittier capture this essence:

> For of all sad words of tongue and pen,
> The saddest are these: "It might have been!"

One pondering point, if treated with the significance it deserves, can make all the difference for one's direction. It can prompt a feeling of accomplishment and well being. Small seeds can produce great moments.

As the music soothed his body, he turned to the album before him for further comfort to his soul

> Thoughts on Your Birthday—
> On this special day, remembered with a tender sigh,
>   The sentiment that fills the heart,
> Like surging water cresting high,
>   Is boundless and a thing apart.
> It recalls the many days and nights
>   Of meaningful and varied association –
> Of direct responses and subtle insights,
>   Climaxing a love in constancy and perpetuation.
> May this wondrous state never cease
>   Or lessen in tempo and in scope –
> And like the slack of a tightly held rope
>   May it, in proportion, always increase!
>   Your Gilbert

> Our 11th Anniversary—
> I well remember that bliss-filled day
> When you and I were joined into one
> My commitment induced in such a way
> As to make hearts joyful and bright like the sun;

Overwhelmed with a sense of triumph and more
Due to your grasping of destiny in your capable
hands,
Shaping events through obstacles galore
Thus evoking my gratitude for all that now stands
Like a statue implanted in nurturing earth,
Representing my everlasting appreciation
And acknowledgement of your immeasurable worth –
All culminating into this event and celebration!
                                    Your Gilbert

SEVEN

Back in what he described as his writing room, Justin gazed out the large windows at the picturesque mountains and the river snaking its way through the valley below. The grandeur of nature on display before his eyes. To be appreciated by all who might take a moment to share in its beauty, its tranquility. There were times such as these that he wished he were a painter rather than a writer. Words are inadequate to capture such a breathtaking, awe-inspiring view. He had really never tried his hand at painting, and he noted in a distant part of his mind to try at some future time to paint this most alluring scene.

Such random, divergent thoughts and enterprises had to be suppressed. The one overriding action and activity was the novel. The occurrences in the story overshadowed all of the mundane actions of his daily life. Sleeping and eating had become secondary. The most troubling aspect had been his losing a grasp of the difference between Justin as the storyteller and Justin as the character of Don in the story. As such, would the believability of the plot be sacrificed if he wavered in favor of what he wished should happen instead of what should really happen? The more the story might meander from the real reactions of actual persons, the greater the chance that the story would lose its appeal. It might become a fantasy, and that is not what he wanted it to be. Not what he felt it had to be.

Estelle entered the room, instantly sensing his immersion in deep thought. The trip had been difficult for her as well. She seemed to feel a new form of weariness. The external battles in the fight for a cause, the frustration of trying to run and keep a multifaceted organization together.

Now, the difficulty with Justin. His mind and heart seemed to be distancing themselves from her, from the family unit, from the home. If she could be sure that it was just the book, and that when the enterprise ended their disturbed life would return to normal, she might be able to cope. But, she was slowly believing that there was a deeper form of disassociation brewing in his unpredictable antics. Justin's wants and potential satisfaction appeared to be growing beyond the reach of her understanding, perhaps even beyond her ability to fulfill them. The inexplicable truism took hold, life really is not simple. The complexity of human beings infiltrates into the basic compartments of one's desires and expectations. The more difficult it becomes to comprehend oneself, it becomes impossible to know others.

Justin looked up at her. "Please sit with me," he gestured with his hand accompanied by a voice unusually weak.

Estelle silently obeyed, clasping his fingers as he offered them to her.

When he resumed speaking, the words came out slowly, hesitatingly. "I sometimes overlook the fact that my undertaking is as hard on you as it is on me."

Tempted to respond, she thought better of it. Let him have his say first.

He continued in measured tones. "Writing a novel has been agonizing. It is a strange twist on reality. It is god-like. I am actually creating life. Each character takes on an existence and a meaning that I bestow on him or her. I wind up feeling the pain of their failures, and rejoice in their successes. Then, defying comprehension, once I have created them it is they who are dictating the story to me. They reveal themselves in my inner thoughts what they want to do in the story, who they want to be, and how they want to be transformed as the plot unfolds. Scary, in a way. It is said that a reader should feel being part of the story and be able to dwell on its meaning long after reading the book. For the author, he should be controlling the story, defining the characters the way he wants them to be. But, I have gone beyond that. The characters are controlling me, and impatiently dictating the story line. They want me to get on with it as if delay dooms their future. I suppose that I am flirting with insanity, and yet that sensation seems to make me write better."

Justin stopped speaking for a moment, a long-off look in his eyes. He gently squeezed her fingers before beginning again. Oddly, she sensed that in some manner he was trying to explain his plight to himself as well as to her.

When he did speak again, it was with increasing effort. "If you are patient with me, I am hoping I can be tolerant of myself. It is quite unfair of me to drag you into this, but being my soul mate you need to share the complete contents of my soul."

"Gladly," was her instant retort. "You would do no less for me."

He gazed deeply into those captivating eyes, the eyes that had not lost any of the allure and brightness that he had been enchanted by when he had met her. At this moment, he had a clear sense of the power and depth of her love for him. "My involvement keeps me totally preoccupied. That you know. At the same time you are an outsider and I, unfortunately, treat you that way. Can you possibly understand that this is the way it must be?"

She measured her words carefully, knowing full well that this was her opportunity to open the door through which she could share this portion of his life. Otherwise, it might well be a door that could never be opened later. "I think only another writer could fully understand such a state of affairs. What I do know is that when I get immersed in my causes, the people who are not swept up in them as I am cannot fully feel the passion to do and to succeed. Since I love you so very much, it is hard to feel shut out. I want to help you, but I am not sure what to do. Even if I knew that, I am not sure I would know how to do it. I recognize that this is your struggle, just as I have my own. Yet, I have always felt that you were behind me in all those undertakings, and I just want you to sense that I am fully behind you with this. Our love has been very special. For me anyway, it had an exceptional beginning that blossomed into more of a happiness and fulfillment that I ever thought would be mine. For all the things that you have done for me, for all of the man that you have been for me, I want to be that pillar behind you that you can lean on when weak and to support you when the tendency exists to buckle under. Will you let me be that pillar for you?"

"I hope you know that I have looked on you as the source of my strength. But, this has become my mountain to climb. My extreme challenge. There is no escaping the practical reality that this is something I have to do by myself. At this point I cannot be satisfied with anything less. It does not mean that my love for you has diminished. In fact, it has increased as I observe how stoic you can be, and I so admire your resolve and perseverance."

"Yes, but you forget that I am not a character in your book. I am a human being with all of the wants and needs that the weakness of my flesh demands. We have not made love since you started the book. I need that closeness, that reassurance of your love for me. Our lovemaking is not just a physical release, it is symbolic of our togetherness. I miss it, and I miss you."

Justin looked at the woman he had fallen in love with at Blantyre University. The love was still there, fervent and true. At this moment, as in the past, he was falling in love with her all over again. Only by virtue of spent youth, its manifestation had changed.

> *Young love is a flame; very pretty, often very hot and fierce, but still only light and flickering.*
> *The love of the older and disciplined heart is as coals, deep-burning, unquenchable.*
> HENRY WARD BEECHER

John Greenleaf Whittier had described it as "the Indian Summer of the heart." She really asked so little from him. While the book was for himself, and an impediment to his surroundings, a gesture of love was for her. How could he deny her?

He drew her close and they kissed with increasing passion. Proving once again that lovemaking is not just for the young. Mature love prompts the same sensations, the full promise of aroused sensual feelings.

Hand-in-hand, they walked to the bedroom. Slowly, he undressed her, renewing the admiration of the still smooth and soft skin on a perfect body. She removed his clothing with adeptness and cunning. Gently, he kissed the hollow of her neck and nibbled her ear lobe. She took hold of his gallant manhood, the sexual thrill rising with the familiar fragrance of his body and the touches on her body that he knew would arouse her.

They sank to the bed and kissed deeply as their bodies touched and molded together. His hand and lips touched each part of her body with patient perfection. He had always been especially gentle with her at these times, and it maximized her arousal. It heightened the moment and preserved it for her heart and mind. Between astute fingers, lips and tongue, he brought her to two powerful climaxes before he sought his own pleasure.

Naked in each other's arms, they slept the night away. Locked in an embrace of revival of spirit and emotion. An act of love as a recommitment to their unity. A resurgence of the significance of their magic together. A very special moment before reality descended on them.

EIGHT

The day was just breaking when Justin entered his writing room to continue his chosen labor. A heavy rain lashed against the picture windows, and the sound added a sense of urgency to his contemplative mood. Extensive imagination bursting to be set free. The mark of the writer. Imagination is a delightful human quality. Children revel in it, but it becomes constrained as they increasingly face the restrictions of society's dictates. Writers can, however, assume the role of child and run amok.

With lap top open, he continued the story in his novel, imagination vented and renewed.

> *Myra: I had almost given up hope of ever hearing from you. I was delighted — no, actually thrilled — to get your email. Old memories, old feelings came rushing in. Your kind attempt to placate my guilt is accepted in the nature it is intended, but without major effect. Of course, since you were the focus of my attention, my memory of your father, especially the role that he played in your life, is dim. I do recall that he was the ruler of the house, but that was common back in those days. In hindsight, you can recognize the damage done, and if I had been the boyfriend I should have been, I might have been able to offset at least part of the debilitating atmosphere he created. The names of your friends also are too distant for me to place with a face or an event. That you have maintained such close associations over all of these years is heartwarming, I am*

sure. For me, I have had no long-term, sustaining friendships. I did re-establish a childhood friendship recently that had extended through the college years. I was able to find him through the Internet. He lives on the West Coast, and we regularly exchange e-mail messages. After getting over the initial disappointment of his divorce to his first wife (I had introduced them), he has remarried to a woman with five children. You might say that his home life has taken an interesting turn, maybe even five turns! He also has custody of the two children from his first marriage. Seven could well be his lucky number! Perhaps you remember him. I cannot recall specifically, but we probably double-dated at times, and he was most likely at many of the parties we had gone to. His name is Dan Afran.

As for me, nothing really exciting or unusual to reveal. I have only been married once, and it is going on to twenty years now. Melanie is a kind, gentle woman. A good human being. The passion long ago left from the coupling. She surmises that the familiarity of so many years together does that between man and wife, but I refuse to accept that as a basic premise. Sure the ardor of the courtship years may wane. Yet, there have to be sparks now and then, not to start a conflagration but certainly a significant blaze of light and warmth. It is not entirely her fault. I realize that. I am much to blame for contributing to the sameness, the dullness of every day life. I am a schedule freak. If the portions of my entire day are not neatly planned out, I am uncomfortable and restless. That leaves little room for spontaneity. Thus, to a large extent, I am inflexible. This is rather perplexing for me as a professed writer. I can conjure up excitement in my writings, including the anticipation of romance with all of its attending emotions. So, why can't I translate it into my real life? What is it that prevents me from changing my restrictive habits, my staid demeanor? One of these days, I really must engage in prolonged self-analysis. Failing at that, I suppose I should see a professional, but I dare say I would drive such a person to the brink before any help would be forthcoming for me. I am a simple man *with so many inner complexities that I defy all of the stereotypes. So, as you can see, you are not the only one who has problems. Others out there are also trying to find their way through the maze. Or, at least, a new approach to needs and wants.*

I have two teenage daughters. I have tried to instill in them a basic sense of humor so that they can laugh away the small stuff. Life is a struggle for them. No different than with so many other youngsters. Mixed signals from adults, from school, from society. Not knowing who to trust. The dilemma of succumbing to peer pressure or asserting a form of individualism. The wanting of a boyfriend without really needing one. The urge to know but not to appear too smart. Caught in perhaps the most uncomfortable position in life — no longer a child and not yet an adult. A mixture of roles which appear overwhelming to sort out. I feel their turmoil. You and I were there once. So have we all.

Now that we have started communicating, my memory has been much keener about times past. It is almost as if the power of concentration transports me back in time. The words of Lyster are quite fitting: "For the memory of love is sweet, though the love itself were in vain. And what I have lost of pleasure; I assuage what I find in pain." And, I certainly hope that these whimsical words of Mark Twain do not come to pass: "When I was younger, I could remember any thing, whether it happened or not; but my faculties are decaying now and soon I shall be so I cannot remember any but the things that never happened." At least about us, you can confirm for me whether the things I remember actually happened and they are not merely figments of my imagination. The longer the duration between an occurrence and its recall, some degree of imaginative reformation takes place either towards the positive or the negative depending on the personal inclination to the person or the event in the images. Two distinct memories linger sharply in my mind. We are walking in the woods. My arm is around your shoulder, your arm is around my waist. The sun is bright, its warmth soaking into our bodies. Spring flowers abound. An array of dazzling colors bringing constant exclamations of delight to your lips. The songs of birds accompany our every step as we make our own trail through the woods. Since we both had been brought up in a city environment, the thrill and exuberance of nature held even a greater emphasis. The magic was contagious. I guide you into a thick grove of pine trees. On a bed of soft pine needles, our naked bodies touch, joined as if a transformation into but one body. It is not merely an act of love. It is a testament to the moment, to the setting, to the miraculous achievement that for no matter how brief a period of time two can be one. Looking back on this, it was the only time I have ever experienced refreshment and rejuvenation from what is an act of simple pleasure. It defies credibility that I gave that up. Abandoned it under a false notion that I had to explore a world beyond that. In fact, that should have been the end of all my explorations. I know it now. How come I could not recognize it then?

The other clear memory is the Sunday rituals. After dinner, with studies completed, I would drive over to your house. We would then drive over to Ashford Park. Sitting in the car, between hand-holding, caresses, ardent kisses, we exchanged thoughts and ideas in what can best be described as a rushing, endless stream. Was there any subject that we did not discuss? Looking back on this, now I realize that then is when I learned that an exchange of thoughts, particularly about people and life, takes one to a realm — to a plateau — unreachable on one's sole devices. I have no doubt that the ability for me to express my thoughts so extensively, to be able to set them down on paper, is due in large part to this gift that you so generously, so openly, so honestly, shared with me. If some one else were to read this, the impression would be that I am portraying you as a goddess. I recognize that you were and are only human. Yet, I am convinced that only when a person is totally relaxed does the true inner self emerge. If nothing else, I reached that stage of complete relaxation with you. Societal factors did not restrict my thoughts, my emotions. Without really knowing it, I was the complete me. I hope that you can look back on that period and as you dwell on that time you can gain a similar insight. Despite the influence of your father, when we were together, there were no parents, no college, no barriers except our own naiveté. At that juncture we were all that we could be. A rather simple conclusion. Yet, I now do believe it fully. Of course, while living it, I had not the foggiest notion of what I had, what we were, and what I was giving up by losing you. Adding greater emphasis to that haunting truism — we never know what we have really lost until it is gone.

Well, I am sure that my ramblings have just about put you to sleep. The sensible thing is not to live in the past but to maximize the present and look to the future. But, I cannot in good conscience say that I have ever been sensible. I gave you up, didn't I? As a hopeless romantic, ramblings camouflage my sensitivities, my weaknesses. For all of the dictates of sensibility, my spirit lives in the past.

Don

Justin sat back and reread the fictitious email message he had just typed out on the screen. Was it all fiction? The happenings to a large extent actually occurred. What parts of the meaning were real or merely parts of an interpretation that he wanted to be true? What was the product of his writer's motivation? Even he could not tell. Not that it really mattered. This was Don's story. Or, was it?

NINE

As soon as she entered the building's laundry room with her pillowcase full of dirty clothes, Lucy recognized the sole individual sitting on the bench reading. It was the man living in the apartment above her apartment. The one who waved to her from the balcony, and whose taste in music reminded her of home. In the instant before he looked up from the open book, she was able to study the handsome, studious face. When he did look up and smiled at her with a broad, warm smile, a strange flutter in her heart instantly spread a warmth throughout her body. She was sure it showed on her face as she felt the warmth surface to her cheeks.

Brandon had looked up to see a petite feminine form enter the small room. A young face accompanied by what seemed to be a child's body clothed in a dark blue sweat suit. As soon as he smiled at her, the blush on her cheeks was evident. The short brown hair framed a slightly freckled face that was a composite of cuteness and prettiness. When she returned his smile, the dimples in her cheeks added another endearing feature. Captivating blue eyes held his attention. He glanced at the washing machine to confirm that his clothes were still churning in the drum, and then returned his gaze back to those riveting blue eyes.

Lucy was the first to speak. The inheritance or emulation of her father's sharp wit had always made her brazen. "You don't have to stare at your clothes in the machine. I doubt if anyone would want to steal them."

Her wide smile accentuated the lightness of the moment. He was quick to pick up on it, and responded in as solemn a tone as he could muster. "My School of Hard Knocks T-shirt is in there. I guard it closely."

"I went there, too. In what year did you graduate?"

" I am still going there, and don't think I'll ever make it out. They won't give me another T-shirt, no matter how long my student stay is."

"Too bad. I graduated with honors. Perhaps, I can tutor you. Your weakest subject must be in politeness. You still haven't invited me to sit down."

"I was going to do better than that. I was going to invite you to read my book for me so that I could watch my wash constantly."

"No wonder you can't graduate. You can't give without taking. You should say if I read your book for you, you will do my wash, clean my apartment, and cook my dinner."

Shrugging his shoulders, he laughed effortlessly. "I just can't get the hang of it. I better take you up on your offer to tutor me." Brandon rose, and his six-foot, two-inch frame towered over Lucy's five-foot height. "On second thought, I am not sure that I want a tutor that I am always looking down on."

Lucy laughed unguardedly. "You better always sit in my presence, then. I am Lucy Post, and I am already looking out for you!"

He extended his hand, and the handshake was natural and nearly familiar. "Brandon Weyland. I am supposed to say that I am pleased to meet you. I do remember that from politeness class, but it seems as if I would have said it without any learning whatsoever."

Instead of sitting, he took the pillowcase and emptied it into an idle machine. She added the detergent, dropped the quarters in the slot, and the machine came to life.

They both sat down. "Actually," she said with a note of candor, "I already know you. I mean, I know something about you."

"How is that?"

"You live above me. You waved at me once when I was out jogging, and thanks to the thin flooring, I have much appreciated the music you play."

"Invading my choice of classics? If I had known, I would have played them even louder."

"It so happens that Shostakovich's Fifth Symphony and Mahler's First are two of my father's favorites. I grew up with them as my background music, my mood enhancement."

"He must be a fine man."

"He definitely is that."

"Mine was too. He died at much too early an age."

"Sorry."

"No need to be. He left me much to remember him by. The shortness of life is not the criteria to measure accomplishments or success as a human being."

"One cannot argue with that. I think you really do not need a tutor. Just a refresher course."

"Is that your specialty?"

"It should be, but I could use one myself. I have already turned stale."

"That is one of the reasons I secretly do not ever want to graduate from the School of Hard Knocks. It is one thing to face reality. It is quite another thing to have to understand it."

She looked at him intently. What a kind statement to make. It revealed to her that here was a man of sensitivity, keenly aware that what she needed most to hear was just that combination of reasonableness and encouragement. In such a brief period of time she had never developed a mental feeling of closeness with another person. The added physical attraction made the impact just that much greater.

Even after the washes were completed, they sat and talked for a long time. Much of the focus was on themselves. Lucy also talked extensively about her parents, as well as the story behind their legendary status at Blantyre. When they reached the subject of their teaching experiences, it was Brandon who came up with the idea of exchanging guest lectures to give the students a different perspective. Lucy thought it was a real good idea, and it might provide just that added spark for her to take control as well as supply an impressive ingredient.

Just before he left her at her door, while handing over the wash bundle he carried for her, he asked if she would want to accompany him on Friday evening to a bohemian coffeehouse he had discovered. Frequented by all sorts of writers, poets and creative listeners, he had found it to be a stimulating place. It was time for him to volunteer to read some poems written by a friend of his from Capitol Hill. Lucy accepted without hesitation.

Back in her apartment, she could barely contain the fluttering in her heart. The warmth that the thought of him provoked soothed her aching spirits. Not only had she made an interesting and stimulating acquaintance, it was a novel experience for her to feel so at ease with a man. Her limited experiences at dating and romance were never like this. They were awkward and strained. With Brandon she felt so at ease. She talked without mental restriction. She could say anything that came to her mind, and in any way that it came out without guarded concern so common before one speaks. It was as if she had known him for a long time, an old friend who would not be offended if she spoke her mind freely. Knowing that her parents had this kind of comfortable relationship, Lucy wondered if this, for the first time in her young years, is love. The experience we all seek to fulfill that special part of our being human. To want another and to be wanted. To share the intimacies. To reach happiness. Whatever it is, she basked in the euphoria of its every sensation. She wished that Friday evening would arrive quickly.

Brandon settled into his chair, an album spread across his lap. As never before, he had just opened up his closet of reservedness to a woman. A door that he had almost come to believe might never be opened. It was more than the sensation that she listened so intently. Her reactions seemed so genuine, so honest. Her words and thoughts were clear and interesting. The description of her life, her philosophy, her goals, were so compatible with his. So many of the women he had thought he might be able to get close to did not turn out that way. Often, he secretly wished they would not talk so much. With Lucy, he could not get enough of her words, spell-bound by the facial expressions that accompanied the genuineness of the concepts. Her engrossing wit captured and held his attention. That he had so spontaneously asked her to share the coffeehouse adventure with him was an especially meaningful sign.

As the soothing tick of the clocks and the varied chimes further mellowed his thoughts, he opened up the album with a new incentive. It was not this time to gain comfort from the expressions or to renew his contacts with a special past. It was to look at the deeper meanings in a way that he might be able to relate to them in his own life. To the discovery of a new, blossoming feeling. To let his father share the thoughts he was having about Lucy.

> *After Three Months—*
> *The quarter year now finished*
> *Has seen an ardor undiminished,*
> *A passion more fiery than before*
> *And delights increasing by the score.*
> *It has known a thirst for joy unquenched,*
> *A faith more firmly entrenched,*
> *Sincere affection ever mounting,*
> *And thrills beyond all counting.*
> *It has seen a love, triumphant, true*
> *March towards a goal still in view,*

A love growing daily stronger
And destined to last much longer.
Love, passion, rapture — all ours,
May there be no surcease to our powers!
                                    Your Gilbert

Depths of Despair—
Away from you I feel a tedium —
Poignant, vibrant and tense,
Like the crescendo of a drum
Beating madly to create suspense.
I'm burdened with a sense of loss
And am inconsolable until,
Crushed in my arms, soft as floss,
You whisper magic words that thrill
And revive my spirit, rekindling the spark
That only flickered like a candle in the dark.
                                    Your Gilbert

TEN

For two smitten hearts, Friday evening finally arrived. Brandon knocked on Lucy's door, and they left hand-in-hand for his jeep. It seemed as if it was one of life's most natural acts. As if they had done this many, many times before. An autumn chill just drew them closer, and while walking they caught up on the endeavors that had transpired since their laundry room meeting.

Lucy was highly animated. Just meeting Brandon had imbued her with a new confidence, and her teaching reflected it. His guest lecture this very morning solidified the new grasp she had on the students. Their attentiveness was now keen, and their aroused interest led to many an interesting question and discussion. Her role as teacher was firmly settled.

She squeezed his hand tighter as they moved along to the parking lot. "Thank you so much, Brandon, for your help this morning."

"It was a pleasure to do it. In fact, I rather enjoyed experiencing the joining of two disciplines. Besides, it is your turn next week. You are not trying to get out of that, are you?"

"No, not at all. One good turn deserves another. Being an outsider to the law, I will just say I am an outlaw."

"Then you have a price on your head?"

"Just to be treated to an entertaining evening in the company of a charming lawyer, one whom I know will not turn into a judge, even though we met on the bench."

"Gee, I sure missed my chance. I was reading and I could have just thrown the book at you."

They laughed in unison. If one were to gaze upon their antics, overhear their conversation, the conclusion would be inescapable. If one believes in that sort of thing — these two were made for one another.

After he opened the car door for her and she settled in the seat, she laughed heartily as he crammed his tall frame into the driver's cramped seat. "You do like to torture yourself, don't you?"

"Yes," he grimaced. "I just can't quite seem to get the hang of this. It has been three years, and each time is as if I am doing it for the first time. But, being a wayward philosopher, I like to think it teaches me a lesson each and every time."

"I just can't wait to hear this one! What lesson, maestro?"

"Tall sometimes wishes for small; small sometimes wishes for tall. Either way, size can be an impediment."

"Ah. One size does not always fit all."

"Your father is the proverb lover. Somehow, when I come across ones that deal with tallness, they tend to stay with me. I never really thought an occasion would arise that I could spout them where it would be so relevant and also have a receptive audience. One is from China — *In shallow waters dragons become the joke of shrimps.* Another is from Denmark — *No man is so tall that he need not stretch and none so small that he need never stoop.*"

"I am a receptive audience as well as a captured one. Now, I need to be a thinking one."

As the jeep rolled along, Brandon would not release her hand. He did not need a reminder that he had found someone very special. A find so precious that he would not want to lose it. The holding of hands thus was a symbol and a promise. A symbol of unity. A promise that what touches us with profound meaning is meant to be enduring.

Lucy had found a new peace with herself. This man unexpectedly had become a vital part of her life. He filled her thoughts, consumed her emotions. Her outlook had heightened to a shimmering optimism. His presence gave her great comfort. Just this touch of her hand in his brought a thrill to her bearing.

The Green Onion was a quaint coffeehouse, modeled after the bohemian coffeehouses of the 50s. Small tables surrounded a circular raised platform frequented by one chair and a microphone. They sat at one of the few unoccupied tables against a wall. Lucy was especially glad it was a smoke-free place. She just could not tolerate cigarette smoke. A stance fortified by her environmental agenda. It pleased her that Brandon also was a nonsmoker.

Subdued conversation filtered through the cozy room. A few people had nodded at Brandon as they came in, a subtle acknowledgement of his becoming a regular inhabitant of this special place. The waitress, a young woman that Lucy guessed could well be a student at the University working for money to cover the educational costs, ambled over to the table. She smiled broadly. "Hi Brandon. I hope this sweet thing is your sister. I can't stand competition for your affections."

"Hi, Nora," Brandon said with flare, "not to worry. This is my mother."

"Now I know where you get your youthful looks," Nora replied with a chuckle.

Brandon gestured elegantly with his hand. "Nora, meet Lucy. Lucy, meet Nora, the most efficient waitress this side of.......the room, anyway. Nora, I am afraid Lucy is the front runner for my heart throbs."

"Nice to meet you Lucy. You are one lucky lady to snare him. I am patient. I'll wait it out. But, I do have to admit you are going to be very difficult to beat out."

"Now, I will have to double my efforts to hold on to him," Lucy said with feigned seriousness.

Nora took out a pad no bigger than a lifesaver. "What can I get for you two lovebirds?"

Brandon knew full well that the pad was just a gesture for tourists. Nora remembered every order down to the smallest whim. "Two hot chocolates, with plenty of whipped cream, and two slices of the Green Onion's fabulous apple pie."

"Back in a flash," Nora said over her shoulder on her trip to the kitchen.

Lucy gazed into Brandon's alluring hazel eyes. "I sure do like a man who takes charge. Of course, my face will break out from the chocolate, the whipped cream will add an inch to my waistline, and the apple pie will have to go a long way to beat out one of my mom's specialties."

"That's why I plan to distract you with fascinating conversation between the lively entertainment soon to be presented by what now appears to be calm inhabitants."

He was right. One by one, a mixture of men and women as if following a set program, went to the chair on the platform and recited a poem, an essay, or just spouted forth some extemporaneous commentary on politics, the college, the economy, or life in general.

The hot chocolate was delicious, and Lucy laughed at the blobs of whipped cream affixing themselves to Brandon's lips. The pie, while not as heaping as her mother's, was tasty and satisfying.

As if on cue, Brandon released her hand, kissing the fingers tenderly, and went to the platform. He settled in the chair and spoke in a low tone into the microphone to the hushed gathering. "Good evening, folks. It is always gratifying to appear before an audience already content with food for the body and the soul. It may even lead me to enough courage at some future time to read one of my own creations. But, since this is actually my first time on center stage, I would like to read two special poems written by a friend that I met on Capitol Hill when I worked there." As if anticipating the reaction at the mention of Capitol Hill, Brandon stopped long enough for the collective boos to be vented. "Believe it or not, there are creative, honest talents in such a staid place. Glenn Logan is a poet extraordinaire. His book of poetry, *Prayers to a Dead God,* has been published and can be found on Amazon.com. I have been the fortunate recipient of additional poems as he writes them. Two recent ones from his prolific mind I thought would be illustrative of both the depth and wit of his talent.

> *LESS AND MORE*
> *I have known the rich, and known the poor,*
> *and most every sort in between, and I have*
> *tried to feel comfortable with them all.*
> *And I have found some to be interesting,*
> *and some not — some deep, some shallow —*
> *some good, and some not, among them all —*
> *no group or class having*
> *any monopoly on human worth,*
> *or dignity,*
> *or goodness.*
> *But overall, over the years,*
> *I have nearly always felt more at home*
> *among those who must labor*
> *than among those who do not — felt*
> *more at home among the running poor*
> *than among the rich, idling*
> *in their Mercedes —*
> *or trying to buy their culture*
> *with a credit card.*
> *I have felt more at home among those*
> *who have been locked out, rather than*
> *among those*

who carefully bar their doors —
and their hearts — more at home
among those who have been jailed
than among those who have jailed them.
I have almost always felt more at home
among those who have struggled,
who have had to struggle,
only to find themselves becoming —
to find themselves to be —
both less and more than they had hoped.

ONE & ONE
He was very ugly,
and she was very fair,
and when they married
everyone who knew them
said they were a very ugly pair.
But somehow Ugly-Fair got by,
and Ugly grew in grace,
while Beauty grew in character,
which is no great disgrace.
Now Ugly's not so ugly,
and though Beauty's not so fair,
despite it all,
they make a lovely pair.

Three hours later, they left. It was one of the most interesting evenings Lucy had ever spent. Sharing it with a special person added just that much more significance to a time she would long remember.

Back at their building, he invited her up to his apartment to see his three prize possessions — the books, the clocks, and the albums of his father's poems. Once inside the door, after helping her off with her jacket, he slowly turned her towards him. They kissed. A deep, soft union of lips and bodies. An inviting act that was natural and fulfilling. It was a very special moment for them. It validated the feelings they had for each other. It was both a culmination and a beginning. It was a recognition that the attraction was more than just a fleeting fancy.

The significance was paramount for him when he encouraged her to open an album and read one of his father's poems. He had not bestowed that privilege on anyone else before.

Lucy opened up to a page at random, and as she read her mind and heart digested the words and beautiful emotions set forth before her. This too was Brandon. That made it even more meaningful.

DEEP THOUGHTS ON 8th ANNIVERSARY
To comprehend love's growth and power,
To recognize the pattern it fashions
Is to view it from a vantage tower,
Soaring high above earth's passions,
From where, like seasons rounding the fruit
And developing it through the year,
Is revealed, for all to see, beyond refute,
The fulfillment of its ripened sphere!
For love that lives until its fruit is known
Procreates itself and lives beyond its own.
Your Gilbert

Lucy rose, went to him and hugged him tightly. They kissed again, as if it were for the first time. "Brandon, please let me stay here with you tonight. It has been such a beautiful evening. I do not want it to end."

"Are you sure, Lucy? I want nothing more, believe me. But, I do not want you to feel pressured in any way."

"I am a virgin. While I thought losing that would be a one-sided act of giving, I do not feel that way now and with you. I will be the recipient of your love. A fair exchange as I see it."

In his bed, he was gentle and deliberate with her. Caressing and kissing her softly all over her body repeatedly. Then, he would hold her firmly, flesh bonding to flesh. Instilling a warm, confident and relaxing love as a threshold and not a barrier. After pleasing her so that the ecstasy of the feelings of her own body produced a new world of pleasure for her, he entered her slowly. Lucy was lost in a new discovery of her being. It was a moment of pure delight, introducing her to the patient passion of loving. The insight was also an outsight. She felt as if she could look deep inside of this beautiful person bound in her embrace. Enchanted by the thrilling vision and entrenched by its meaning, she now understood what her parents had together. Two lives are separable but have the capacity to be as one. It was not an evening she would long remember. It was a night she would never forget.

ELEVEN

Estelle ran excitedly into the writing room. She could barely catch her breath, and Justin looked up from the laptop not quite knowing what to make of it. The broad smile on her face was the harbinger of good news. He awaited the pronouncement.

"Justin, darling, you must come and read Lucy's email."

"I can tell by the way you are beaming that this is something I would like to know. Has she been awarded the Nobel prize for environmental science? Won a beauty contest? Flunked her first student?"

"Better than all that.......combined!"

"Oh, my!"

"Lucy is in love."

"This I have to read. She is hallucinating again."

He accompanied her to her desk in the corner of the study. The computer screen revealed the message. He sat down at the computer station, took off his reading glasses just long enough to verify that they were clean, and read the message slowly. He wanted to digest all of the words, knowing full well there would be an extended discussion about it.

> *Dear Mom and Dad —*
> *Another scientific principle bites the dust! Lightning has struck the same place twice! Just as you two fell in love here at Blantyre, so have I. I just had no idea that being in love could be such a glorious event, such a magnificent sensation. I am totally uplifted. I look out onto the world*

that I once only saw as harsh and insensitive and all I see now is a warm and hospitable place. And, the object of this love? Don't laugh — or smirk —he is a lawyer. Actually, an international lawyer, and he teaches here as well. In fact, his apartment is just above mine. You will certainly not believe this. I hardly did at the time, but the music I first heard coming from up there was Shostakovich's Fifth and Mahler's First. Dad, that has to endear him to you despite his lawyer label! His name is Brandon Weyland. We met, so unexpectedly, in the laundry room, and hit it off right away. He is bright, responsive, attentive, witty, and TALL. I could go on and on about him. I can't wait for you to meet him and to discover the qualities that abound in and about him. We have gone out to an artsy coffeehouse, and he read some poems there written by a friend of his. Later, he let me read some love poems that his father had written to his mother. They are both gone now, but he has such wonderful memories of them that his face just glows when he speaks of them. Yes, here is one man brought up in a loving environment to match my loving home, my endearing childhood. That alone could and would be a binding thread. But, there is more, so much more! At his suggestion, we have exchanged guest lectures in each other's classes. That has added a substantial dimension for my students as well as for me. I did not want to overly concern you, but I had been struggling in the role of teacher. I just did not seem to be able to connect with the students. Brandon's surge of interest in me, as well as the appearance he made before my classes, were just the right combination to right the situation. He has bolstered my ego and confidence and brought me around to a healthy attitude and with a substantial result. How can I not help but love a man like this one? Mom, you can especially relate to this. I have yet to discover a single negative thing about him. I know that he is just human, and there must be some frailty, some weakness lurking in the shadows, but I just can't imagine what it might be. Whatever it is or they are, they would pale in comparison to his virtues. I haven't even come to the best part yet. He feels

the same way about me! Because of you both, I have a happy life. My love for and with Brandon has carried this to a new dimension. I am one lucky person. A loving home, and now a man who loves me as a woman and as an equal, and with whom I am now experiencing what you two have found together —that the relationship between a man and a woman can be the ultimate human fulfillment. I know that you are saying to yourselves that this is so sudden. I certainly didn't plan it this way, or even ever dared to dream that such an epic event could happen to me. I have been, as you so well know, withdrawn. There is just no denying this major development in my being. It just happened, and am I glad that it did! I can't wait for you to meet him. Since he has no family, and since my family is so much a part of me, it is a given that he will love you. I just know that you will love him as well. My heart is so large that I can afford to keep part there with you and part with him. I love you both dearly
— Lucy

Justin leaned back and smiled at Estelle. "Wow! Where did our little girl go? I am not quite sure I am ready for this, but I better get up to speed. It sounds awfully serious."

Estelle moved over and sat effortlessly on his lap. The soft kiss on his neck lingered in the quietness. "It brings back some wonderful memories for me. She is living the very same sensations I experienced with you. In a way I am reliving it now through her. I was so concerned that she had never had a serious boyfriend. I had worried that perhaps somehow we had instilled in her subtle barriers to not being satisfied with ordinary people, common events. I am especially pleased that either I was wrong or this Brandon has qualified under demanding criteria. Either way, as you say, she is no longer our little girl."

"What makes it particularly serious in my eyes is that she is not asking for our advice. She is just telling us how it is."

"How should we respond?"

"If you leave it up to me, I would joke my way through it so I would not have to face it squarely. Therefore, I am deferring to you, my dear and wise angel, to give her our tentative blessing and a low-key encouragement."

"Just what I had in mind, doctor."

"Settled. Take two aspirins and call me in the morning. Either you will feel better, or your call will wake me up from this dream." Justin paused for a thoughtful moment. "You had better throw out a proverb or two. Otherwise she will think there is something wrong about any response."

"Sounds about right to me. Do you want to make one up........or are the wheels turning in that sparkling brain to extract the genuine item?"

"Sort of depressing to have a woman know me so well. Let's give her the best of both worlds. A made-up proverb just as she would expect, and then a real one to keep her guessing about the extent of our reaction. How is this one for the imaginary — *True love can only be found in a man picked out by a young woman's parents.*" He paused long enough to assure himself it was phrased just right. "For the true one, you can select one of these:

Love, pain, and money cannot be secret; they soon betray themselves. [SPAIN]

Man, woman, and love created fire. [SPAIN]

Love has produced some heroes but even more idiots. [SWEDEN]

If love is a sickness, patience is the remedy. [CAMEROON]

Wait until the tree has fallen before you jump over it. [THAILAND]

Estelle pondered for a brief moment. "As usual, they are all good. Why not saturate her mind? The message should be clear — love is wonderful but it can be a problem as well. She should be extra cautious before she gets carried away."

"Even if that is advice you did not follow yourself?"

"If you will remember, kind sir, I had no one to listen to. Only my heart spoke to me. Luckily, it spoke the truth."

"As long as we are talking about love and relationships, let me ask you this. Do you ever regret not having more relationships before settling into a life with me?"

"Not for an instant," was her quick retort. "I was convinced you were right for me, and confident that I had found my life's fulfillment in you.

Why look further?"

"The heart, however, can function at its best with romantic experience."

"True, in some cases. In others, the newness, the freshness of the feeling as well as the enchantment, are too precious to subjugate for pure numbers."

"Then, you do not think we should emphasize to her that she is young, inexperienced in affairs of the heart, and vulnerable to infatuation?"

"Do you think she would listen?"

"Listen, yes; follow, no. She is head strong as her mother is and will do what she wants. In spite of this Brandon's good taste in music, women, and potential in-laws, there is little we can really say that will sway her. She is her mother's daughter! I know that being hurt is a vital part of growing up, but I do wish we could either brace her for such a possibility or, at least, soften any such blow."

Estelle kissed his cheek, her lips lingering on the flesh. "Lucy is our love-child. She has been nurtured in love and has a high level of esteem and perception. Whether this love she has found is a lasting one or not, she will emerge even better than she was before."

Justin held her tightly. He whispered in her ear. "I hope you are right. Each and every event is a reminder to me what a wonderful woman you are and how very much I love you."

"Ah, an insight for you to the way that I feel about you every moment of every day."

Their kiss was deep, lasting and sensual. A calmness descended over their clutched forms. A singular emotional entity. These were the magical times when their unity captivated and subjugated their individuality. They could wish no more for Lucy and Brandon than they discover the same charmed circle. And, if so, that they know how to care for it.

TWELVE

There just had to have been a simpler time in his life, but Justin could not remember when that might have been. Complex conflicting thoughts and feelings had been with him for so long that it had become particularly difficult to maintain adequate perspective. If nothing else, this state of affairs was amply reflected in the trials and tribulations of the main character in his novel, Donald.

Added to this already perplexing mixture was an inner turmoil concerning Lucy's pronouncement of found love. While he did not want to convey his initial trepidation to Estelle, it was festering within him. Lucy is too young, too inexperienced to keep her heart and mind in unison. Or, was it just the shock that his influence as the primary male figure in her life had been usurped by a stranger? This dilemma needed to be resolved quickly. Yet, he was helpless to calm the spirits of Donald in a fictional scenario. How could he possibly find a balance in a real situation begging for resolution? What loomed so large in the face of his situation was that he knew that all of the ingredients for a satisfying life were within his reach, so why was he so restless? What key element was lacking in his own make-up? Ample ingredients for frustration and despair. To avoid that kind of self-confrontation, he resumed work on the novel.

It seemed as if Donald's life was adrift on a lonely sea. The meaning surrounding his job, his family, and the very existence he had nurtured over the intervening years were in extreme peril. He was living on two plateaus. One, his college years with Myra; the other, the renewed contact with her.

These phases overshadowed every thing else. As such, as the days dragged into a week since her last message, emotional torture racked his being. At long last, a message arrived.

Don —Your book was beautifully written. Your email messages are also wonderful. In spite of your statement about not making me out to be a goddess, that is the way I come across. Your writer's imagination has carried you away! I am afraid it sweeps me away as well, off to a place that I should not be in and with an ideology that I can scarcely live up to. It is flattering to know that you look upon me with such allure. But, that is not really me. My past deeds, particularly the truly minimal part I played in your life, do not really deserve such praise or elevation. While I am captivated by it, the heroine in your book is not me and can never be me. To be frank, you would be disappointed by the Myra that I am. Besides my teaching and the relationship with my daughter, I am not the picture of strength and wisdom that you paint so eloquently. I am a simple woman who has a bad track record of failing in personal relationships with men, including the relationship with you. If I were really what you portray me as, surely I would have been able to hold on to you. I would have been able to make you see the folly in leaving me. I would have succeeded in conveying to you the vision that a life with me was to be your real quest for the rainbow's end. If the truth be known, I let you slip away just so that I would not have to put my character to a test of will and action. Hurt and disappointment were the qualities I was most accustomed to. It was almost as if I constantly wished them upon myself. Now, perhaps late in life, that I am putting my tattered esteem together into what resembles a reasonable whole, this effort consumes all of my attention. I hope that you can understand how very important this is to me right now. Even though it is still a mystery to me in so many ways, I do love life. I am no different than millions of others. I do not deserve the halo that you bestow upon my head. In fact, I think it harms me and my plans to be cast that way. Yes, I remem-

ber some very wonderful times we spent together. They had that extra meaning because you were my first boyfriend. Young people read into new experiences such worldly dimensions. A first love is so serious, so frantic. But, that is all it was! You should not place any greater significance to it than that. It was an emotional experience in the formative stage of our lives. Nothing more, and nothing less. I loved the book, and I will cherish it not only as a beautiful piece of prose but because I was the source of inspiration for a great talent to surface. I urge you to reconsider getting it publicly published so that the whole world can enjoy the quality of your writing and the probing thoughts you convey in it. Young people will benefit greatly from the message in your fine work of literature. Being a teacher, I see too many youngsters floundering. Reading your story can reveal to them that a sense of being lost is a natural part of growing up and that it can really be a tool for self-discovery. I had delayed in responding to you unsure of what I wanted to say. At first, I thought we could build on the past and become friends. Sensing you seek more than that, I am not prepared for that. In fact, I now feel strongly that even a friendship would be unwise. I doubt if you would be satisfied with that. Selfishly, I think it would sidetrack me from the progress I am making for the first extended period of my life in which I feel good about me. Also, it would devastate me to know that I might be instrumental in breaking up your marriage and distancing yourself from your daughters. Perhaps, for the first time in my life I am prepared to do a noble act. It greatly adds to my feeling of self-worth. I am confident that I am doing the right thing for you as well as for me. Donald, please do not try to communicate with me again. I will not respond. Let us leave this as a moment where our paths crossed, and in a pleasant interlude we were able to look back on our trips to distant points and reminisce about some shared pleasant memories. Our paths need to now veer off in different directions. And, when we have arrived at whatever ultimate destinations are fated for us, I know I will look back at this crossing as a meaningful and sincere point in my travels. I feel it will be the same for you. I am sure that this is the right decision. Please accept it in the spirit in which it is offered. Go on with your writing, proceed with your own life. There are those who depend on you.

Forever grateful,
Myra

Justin's hands trembled. His breathing was short. Scarcely could he believe that he had written a rebuff to Donald from Myra. The plot had been fixed in his mind since the beginning. His focus had always been clear on its ultimate execution. Donald and Myra were to continue exchanging messages, each successively drawing them closer together. Then they were to arrange a meeting, finally realizing that they had not only become reacquainted through their writing but that they had also gotten to know each other well and liked what they had found. Then, they go on to recapture the love they once had. Proving to the entire world that such a monumental event is possible. So, how did this turn of events happen? Who had willed it? What did it mean?

Visibly and emotionally shaken, Justin walked to the window. Staring at the tranquil valley for a long time, gradually his body relaxed and breathing became effortless. Enlightenment is the door to understanding. Myra's denial was not for Donald. It was for him, Justin. It was the closure that he had sought with Rosalind. It was Justin speaking through Myra. It was the mechanism for lifting the guilt that had hung over him for so many years. It was a catharsis. It was the kind of meaningful inner transformation that he needed but would probably never fully understand how it had happened. He rushed off to explain these surging events to Estelle.

THIRTEEN

After reading her parent's email messages four times, Lucy shared their mixed contents with Brandon. It was a good reflection of their humor, the great love they have for her, and the high degree of confidence in her instincts and decisions. They were just the kind of response she had anticipated. Encouragement tinged with a loving reminder to exercise caution. An expressed observation to fully note the extent of her own feelings rather than a direction aimed at the exercise of judgment in the selection of the object of her love.

She wondered what their reaction would be to the latest development. She had moved into Brandon's apartment to be with him at all times. Her rented furniture did not have the same meaning as the possessions that were part of his being. It took no effort on her part to feel welcome and comfortable in these surroundings. In fact, she wanted to share all of the aspects of living with this loving man, including the day-to-day chores as well as the moments of sweet passion when their lovemaking led to great satisfaction on both their parts. His attentiveness and constant displays of affection gave her mind and heart great comfort. Her happiness had reached a new dimension.

Whenever she did go down to her apartment, she would stop at the refrigerator to fully partake of the paper held on to the door by two magnetized teddy bears. A love poem from Brandon. Not only was there the significance in the words, it was the first love poem she had ever received. She knew it was the first of many emanating from the gentle heart that bestowed such thoughts upon her. Brandon had inherited his father's genius, and she was the inspiration that had brought it to the surface as a mighty geyser.

My Lucy – The Spring of My Life
  In Spring, buds appear on each barren branch,
  Birds nest in celebration of the nesting season;
  Animals and plants leap to life not by chance
  But as if each surging moment has its reason.

  As if my life had always been confined to Winter's hue,
  When I met Lucy, I entered the Spring of my existence;
  My heart and mind told me it is natural to grow with you,
  And I have surged and blossomed as if by instinct.

  Now in the Spring of my life with your love to hold,
  It leads me to love you with an increased fervor;
  There is no fear of emptiness or of growing old,
  As I am protected by a heart embrace forever.

  The day I met you my life's Spring was initiated,
  All of the world is flowing in an enchanting design;
  The purpose of my life is now well illuminated,
  The comfort and meaning of togetherness is mine.

  Lucy, enter with me into the garden of delight,
  Let us nurture what we have surprisingly found;
  The door of all tomorrows is open to the light,
  And our travel together is eternally bound.

Lucy thought it would take some coaxing to have Brandon go home with her at Thanksgiving. Her parents were receptive to the idea. When Brandon agreed as soon as she mentioned it, that left her even further elated. In fact, his constant show of flexibility had already taught her a valuable lesson. Trees bend so they do not break in an ill wind. Being stubborn or fixed in a position or opinion leaves little room for balanced judgment. Once a flexible outlook and an openness to a change of ideas takes hold, how easy it is to adjust to new ways. Even for an admission that one might be wrong in a stance once taken. There can be more than one way to reach conclusions. Even the questions or issues may be subject to a number of interpretations.

She recalled the aura she felt when he lectured her class. Self-confidence exuded from his being and the grasp he had of the subject matter. Just the right blend of humor and personal observations held the group's attention. She, herself, was spellbound. Having no experience or interest in law as a subject for study, she clung to the expression of rules and principles as he traced their development and application to many of the leading stories in the newspapers. She had already learned from him on many fronts. Law and environmental science were a good match. A better match was their two personalities and characters.

They cooked and cleaned as a team, and tended to each small task as a joint effort. She even took great enjoyment in winding the clocks and learning about the different clock companies and clockmakers. Most of them were from the famous and some of the obscure clockmakers that had clustered in Connecticut in the Nineteenth Century. Some had beautiful reverse paintings on the glass on the doors. Brandon explained the true nature and value of antique clocks. Each one has a unique quality, and they are a fine investment since they appreciate in beauty and value as they age. Besides being highly decorative, they are faithful servants and friends for all time and times.

One clock had an especially interesting story behind it. While not an antique clock but merely a reproduction, Lucy listened with fascination at the story behind its maker. Brandon had an Elmer Stennes steeple clock, a handsome clock to admire. It had become a collector's Mecca not only because of its quality but also because of the infamy of Elmer Stennes. He had been convicted of murdering his wife, and spent only four years in prison. During that period, prison officials actually let him continue to make clocks. After his release, he remarried and was then murdered himself.

The lovemaking equaled the other properties of the union. Brandon so enjoyed awakening Lucy's body to new sensations, and his gentleness guided her in directions she had never dreamed existed. Thrilling actions tested her youthful stamina to extreme limits. For Brandon as well, he had never experienced a love-entwinement of such great proportions. It was not the satisfaction of the body as much as the contentment of the mind that enchanted him. Engulfing her small frame in his arms cast an impervious blanket over them. Her body became an extension of his own. Pulsating emotions in tandem, precisely coordinated with the beating of their hearts.

Fear less, hope more;
Whine less, breathe more;
Talk less, say more;
Hate less, love more;
And all good things are yours.
[SWEDEN]

What Lucy liked best was awakening in the middle of the night to discover that she was not alone. Her engulfed body cradled in his tender grasp. A warm feeling of safety and security. Inexhaustible. Invaluable. In perpetu.

FOURTEEN

Estelle and Justin puttered around the kitchen. This was to be a special Thanksgiving feast. It had been nearly three months since they had seen Lucy. Brandon was coming with her, and it would be their first introduction to the new prominent person in her life. Both readily admitted that they were a bit nervous.

The turkey roasting in the oven filled the house with an inviting aroma. Justin, trying not to dwell on the forthcoming meeting, was intent on preparing one of Lucy's favorite dishes. Sweet potatoes blended with orange juice, to be topped with marshmallows and popped under the broiler for a few minutes just before serving to allow the marshmallows to get gooey.

Estelle gently placed the palm of her hand on Justin's cheek. "Our son is coming. The one I never could give you."

He covered her hand with his own, and moving her palm to his lips he let it linger there as if the gesture would speak its own substance. "My family has always been complete. Lucy made up for a dozen daughters and sons. But, if this Brandon turns out to be a fraction of what Lucy has portrayed, the family will just be further enriched."

"I suppose we are predisposed to like him for Lucy's sake. A far cry from the reaction of my parents on that Christmas long ago when you came for dinner."

"I remember that far too well. Your presence was a loving buffer. As I look back on it, that was really a very small thing for me to do for you. How little you have demanded from me over the years! No wonder you are the apex of my mental and emotional fortunes."

Estelle smiled that wondrous, heart-melting smile. "Keep up that kind of sweet talk and my eyes will be puffy from weeping. You don't want Brandon to think I am a puffball, do you?"

Justin drew her into a close, meaningful embrace. "No, that will never do. Puffed pastry, maybe; puffy eyes, no."

With a degree of reluctance, she parted from the bodily contact but kept a hand on his shoulder. "And a couple of turkeys, as well."

Justin laughed without restraint. His entire being had settled into a calm pool of soothing water since abandoning the book. In an undefinable small way, he would have liked to have finished it. Perhaps, it was just not finishing a task he had started, just as the way it had been by being prevented to complete the seminar at Blantyre. The story was a good one. Unique in a way. A book within a book within another book. He had now to focus on new ventures. After they would return from their upcoming two-week trip to Mexico and Guatemala after the first of the year he would revisit the agenda formulating in his mind to satisfy the fresh rebirth of his intellectual meandering. Not a have-to-do list. A want-to-do list.

Estelle returned to the preparations, her mind adrift on swift moving currents. Mentioning her parents and that Christmas fiasco so long ago when they first met Justin and their hostility towards him led her to focus on the past. This present moment loomed even larger in the light of that memory. She so much wanted to like Brandon and for him to like them. Then, there was the excitement of this trip to Mexico and Guatemala, the first to Guatemala as an especially environmentally degraded nation. A rare opportunity for her to carry her message and AGE's principles into the thick of a burgeoning problem arena. To get out from the large cities and into the lowlands to be an actual mover to help ward off a project threatening great damage to the ecostructure. At the very core of her quest for a better world.

Lucy and Brandon stood before the door. One of the strange developments in this thing called life is that a small, routine matter may turn into a dilemma. For Lucy, whether to use her key to open the door or to ring the bell. As if sharing her quandary, Brandon offered an intimate solution in a typically jovial fashion tinged with a serious message. "A door never opened leaves you without the knowledge of what lies beyond it. Since I can smell turkey cooking, it is also going to deprive my yearning stomach of sustenance. I suggest that you ring the bell. It is not a clock, but the chime will announce our presence on the hour."

She kissed him lightly on the cheek. "A timely suggestion. Time also for us to be insiders. No wonder I love you so much. Our love can even open this door one way or another."

"Then you had better ring the bell twice. They are getting two for the price of one."

The door opened right after the second ring. Lucy rushed into the offered embrace awaiting them, just as Justin gushed, "She had to wear out the bell twice, certain that the old folks are going deaf."

With all of the theatrical antics she could muster, Lucy announced, "And here, my dear parents, is the man of my dreams. My beloved, Brandon Weyland."

Brandon bent down to warmly hug Estelle's small frame, so duplicative of Lucy's stature. " I may be beloved to her, but please call me Brandon."

The men shook hands, and after coats were hung in the guest closet, they all headed for the kitchen.

"We entertain family in the kitchen," Estelle chirped gleefully. "I hope you don't mind."

"Not at all," Brandon responded with gusto. "It certainly enhances my appetite to be at the very source of meal preparations."

Justin inserted quickly, "He must be a lawyer. It sounded real good, but I did not understand a word of it. I think he was trying to say that it is o.k."

Lucy gave Brandon the grand tour of the house, and as small as it is she had an interesting story to identify each room. They lingered in the writing room. While gazing out at the vista that Brandon could especially enjoy, she recounted the many instances when the room had taken on a life of its own. The expanse of the picture windows had a way of expanding the mind of an occupant. Windows, contrary to doors, need not be opened to experience and be affected by what lies beyond them.

"This is the repository of much intellectual thinking," Lucy exclaimed holding Brandon's hands close to her sides.

"Yes, I can readily understand it. On this spot, I am a midget in the land of giants."

"Do not feel intimidated. There is wonderful magic in this place. You will grow into it and because of it."

Holding her from behind, they watched the night slowly settle on the mountain and the valley. Lucy had watched this transformation countless times. It was still an invigorating spectacle. New mysteries seemed to lurk in the growing shadows. Even the darkness offered a spellbinding enchantment.

At the dinner table, the succulent culinary delights helped to foster lively conversation. Discussions vacillated between the inane and the deeper issues of the day, and always the thread of genuine humor held overreactions in check. Common viewpoints were shared in abundance, and the mutual admiration between the parents and the newcomer grew in degrees. This pleased Lucy no end. The vitality and reason for her being were all around this table. She clung to Brandon's hand whenever there was a break from eating and she was not helping her mother with the serving. Justin and Estelle were well impressed by this young man, particularly by the attention and consideration he extensively bestowed on Lucy.

Only once did Brandon seem to cast an ominous note on his words. When the elder Posts mentioned their forthcoming trip to Mexico and Guatemala, Brandon recounted the extensive hearings that the Senate Foreign Relations Committee had held before his departure reviewing the foreign aid assistance to Guatemala. Not wanting to sound overly alarming, he cautioned them to be observant and constantly attentive while there. Amidst a volatile political situation, Guatemala had the highest crime rate in Latin America. Violent crime is a serious and growing concern due to endemic poverty, an abundance of weapons, a legacy of societal violence, and a dysfunctional judicial system.

Discussions continued after they had settled in the living room long after the meal was over, the dishes washed and tucked away. A group effort in consumption and then refurbishment.

Exhausted by the drive and the long day, Lucy and Brandon shortly fell asleep in Lucy's bed entwined in each other's arms. Her bed had never felt so fulfilling. It had been a satisfactory and rewarding day, and there were ample reasons to be relaxed and content.

The sleeping arrangements were consistent with the tenure of the household. Lucy had just taken Brandon to her bedroom. Justin and Estelle merely accepted it as Lucy's wish. They had never been prudes, and they certainly were not going to start now. It was in a way a natural act. One that they would have done in a similar situation back when the love of their youth would have dictated their not being apart when not really necessary.

FIFTEEN

The plane landed in Mexico City, the first leg of their trip, just as the sun was setting. Estelle clasped Justin's hand with a tight grip until the plane's wheels were firmly on the landing field. At the special invitation of the President of Mexico, Estelle was to make a speech as part of the so-called Mexican environmental crusade. They looked towards a partnership with private groups with international influence, such as the Alliance for a Green Earth. As its lead person, Estelle Post was a key speaker at the dinner to be held the following evening.

Mexico City's air quality was among the worst in the world, and even with the legislative efforts providing for tax incentives for the purchase of pollution control equipment as well as other general provisions providing for ecological equilibrium and environmental protection, little improvement had yet been made. A ten-year program was being launched to include such initiatives as developing clean taxis and small buses to reduce urban emissions, improving the environmental infrastructure, and strengthening environmental planning and administration in the northern border regions. AGE had lent financial support and had sent a staff to work with local officials in launching these programs. The Mexican government adopted many of AGE's creative pollution fighting policies, and there was unison of the cause to prevent further large-scale environmental damage.

Settled in the hotel for the night, despite the major undertakings that lay ahead on this trip, here there were a few untroubled moments to rehash the warm, receptive feeling that had been generated by Brandon on the family.

Sufficient time once again to congratulate themselves on the wonderful job they had done in raising Lucy. That had to be among their greatest accomplishments.

Estelle lightly touched his cheek as they lay together in the bed. The overhead fan was the only noise in the room. Justin was unusually quiet, and it made her think of the fiery intellect of his youth. Such a dashing, leadership role he had played. An entry into her life at a most problematic time and, in effect, launching that life. She could not have done better in having a mate even if she had conjured one up.

"Is there anything wrong, sweetheart?" Her voice trembled ever so slightly.

It was a prolonged moment before he responded. His tone was slow, deliberate. "No, not really. I just sense I am at an awkward juncture of my life. On one hand, I feel as if I have accomplished much. On the other hand, I sense that I could or should do so much more."

"A natural feeling, I would surmise."

"Natural for you, still tackling the problems of the world."

"But not able to do so without my navigator to lead me though stormy seas to tranquil waters."

The comfort of an accustomed embrace. They fell asleep locked in each other's arms. More than an act of mere acceptance. A display of shared tolerance. Above all, a tribute to an enduring emotional partnership that had led to so many tangible results from the mutual efforts of mind and body.

The speech was well received, and Estelle was besieged by officials and members of the scientific community for extended and detailed discussions. With Justin at her side, her animated expressions and obvious grasp of the matter at hand duly impressed them all. The Mexican President basked in her visual and oral demeanor as if it too was an accomplishment to the credit of his leadership. He stayed close to participate at opportune moments.

The trip to Guatemala was not to be as promising. There had been ample time during the stay in Mexico to digest all of the briefing papers they had on this enigmatic country, as well as the numerous reports prepared by the research staff of the Alliance on the deforestation situation they were headed to make an impact on. The AGE briefing book summarized the overall dilemma quite well.

Before the Spanish conquest in the Sixteenth Century, Mayan civilization flourished throughout much of Guatemala. In fact, more than half of the current Guatemalans are descendants of indigenous Mayan nations. Guatemala was freed of Spanish colonial rule in 1821. During the second half of the Twentieth Century, there were a number of military and civilian governments. A thirty-six year guerrilla war that had led to the death of more than 100,000 people and created more than one million refugees, ended in 1996. Many remote areas are unsafe for tourists.

In Guatemala, 1.620 square kilometers of tropical rainforest are destroyed each year. Since 1960, 54% of the nation's forest cover has been removed. Domestic and global implications are dire. Most Guatemalans rely on firewood as their sole energy source and lumber as their primary building material. Global warming from the lack of trees and burning of fossil fuels has worldwide implications. Migrating songbirds are declining because they fly to Central America and then die because there are too few trees to nest in.

Pedro Gonzales, who was to be their driver and interpreter for the trip to and stay at the field site, met them at the Guatemala City airport. He seemed much too young for such an assignment, and Justin and Estelle were a bit uneasy from the start. It was evident that the time in this poor country was going to be a series of compromises. They piled their limited belongings in the bed of the old truck and crunched together next to Pedro.

As they made their way along rugged roads, squalor was evident all along the way. Environmental crises just a part of the problematic equation. Small straws to clutch at. Not much better than an empty hand.

Upon arriving finally, dirty and weary, at the Rio Dulce area, they were greeted by Domingo Sanchez, the head of the meager efforts to stem the deforestation calamity. He gave them a quick tour of the feeble efforts in place. It would be a miracle if this American woman could inspire the task so necessary for the future of the nation and its people. He had just about given up. Between the poverty and the gangs of desperados who swayed the course away from a long-range goal to a first priority of staying alive, words did not save trees.

Staying with a local family in a squalid mud hut, Estelle and Justin experienced first-hand the barest essentials of living. One meal a day of bread and beans, and no sanitary resources. There was some doubt they could last out the remaining time there. But, even though the project was closer to a dream than a reality, Estelle had a way of convincing people of the urgency of the situation. Her confident presence and voice, filled with conviction, were persuasive in any language. After the passage of the days marked by hardships and a sense of futility, she had actually begun to make a dent in the local mind set, much to Domingo's amazement.

Yet, their gringo presence was resented by many of the local people. An air of restlessness hung over them. Some attitudes were overtly hostile. Roving bands of criminals had all of the villagers on edge. This was an ever-present threat. At any moment, all that they had could be taken from them.

The night before Estelle and Justin were to leave became the nightmare that had lingered in the minds of the locals. Under the cover of darkness, a drunken horde descended on the village. They shot wildly in the air and at whatever they saw moving, mercilessly beating or killing all who stood in their way. They burned and pillaged the buildings, no matter how meager the structures might be. It resulted in a massacre of tragic proportions. The gringos, Justin and Estelle Post, were an especially easy and compulsive target. It seemed as if the gang took special pride in killing them and burning their bodies. An empty statement for all but themselves.

Knowing that they were about to be killed presented no enlightenment to Justin and Estelle. Cruelty to others, particularly those there to help the unfortunate people and prospects of their country under great stress, defied all rationality. They died clutching each other with the last vestige of the strength in their bodies. Death was mercifully quick. No time for a last vocal expression of love. No time to show the thought and concern of what and who they were and what was being left behind. All spirits crushed. Good intentions squandered in the dirt. Deeds left undone. Words unsaid.

A scream pierced the night. A fervent call to humanity to arise and forever prevent such tragedies. The human animal at the lowest of its bearing and potential. A victim is the same all over the world.

At birth we cry; at death we see why
[BULGARIA].

SIXTEEN

It was days later when Lucy received the tragic news. It was common not to hear from her parents for days on end when they were on a trip, particularly to a remote area. When Jim Harworth from the Alliance called, she was totally unprepared for such a shock. There were no details. All that he knew was that her parents had been killed in a guerilla raid on the village. It was Brandon who was able to get more particulars from a contact at the Department of State. The grisly incident was now supposedly under investigation by Guatemalan officials and United States personnel were not yet allowed on the scene. The scant news reaching the diplomatic corps in Guatemala City was to the effect that of a population of over 400 in the village, a preliminary survey indicated that more than half had been killed, including women and children. The village had been plundered and extensively burned. Many of the bodies were burned beyond recognition. Early estimates were that the bodies of her parents would probably never be identified or recovered.

The tears flowed endlessly. Her sobbing body would have collapsed repeatedly had not Brandon's strong embrace held her together. It was the feeling of emptiness that staggered her the most. As much as she was her own whole person, a part of her now was gone. Death of a loved one is difficult enough when it is expected. A sudden death is cruel and devastating for the loved ones left behind.

Besides the comfort blanketed upon her by Brandon, Lucy was able to find the most solace in Brandon's father's poems. The elegant words and romantic impressions were transposed to her parent's loving relationship.

Poignant insight to the fact that death may take the life but the love fostered by that life endures. It can be in a written poem left behind or merely in a single memory. Lucy had her parents' books, their letters, their possessions, and a string of memories to tie her to their lives throughout what might remain of her own life.

Voraciously, she read and reread the poetry, grasping at the strength and the dignity it offered.

WHEN YOU ARE AWAY
I love you in the North
As I loved you in the South;
I love you on Winter's bleak days
As well as in the Sun's warm rays;
I love you day and night
Be they dismal or be they bright –
But at this moment, when you're away,
These expressions only partly convey
The depth and scope that can only be clear
If I could whisper them into your ear.
Your Gilbert

MUTTERINGS OF GRATITUDE
Since you have become my darling wife
I have tasted the sweetest fruits of life.
I have had new vistas revealed to me;
I have had new beauties impressed on me.
I have realized more and more whereof
Comes the lyric majesty of love.
To you I owe the full success
Of our unprecedented happiness;
To you I owe the bliss inherent in
A mutual regard and high esteem – akin
To pleasure gained from gratified desires
Maintained by the burning of inner fires.
Your Gilbert

THOUGHTS FOR THE 19th ANNIVERSARY
There is no yardstick existing to measure
The infinite, exquisite pleasure.

The utter completeness of love fulfilled
With which my heart with joyous cadence is filled.
It is like some haunting, wondrous melodies
Wherein we have been admitted to their mysteries;
To realize with awe, you and I are of the favored –
A privilege to be ever treasured and slowly savored.
Thus fortified, when waters seem troubled,
There is spirit, and character and effort redoubled
To compensate for a failure to reflect perfection
In the course of human events and their reflection.
When times are tempest-tossed with which to reckon
A promise always seems to beckon –
Life's bits of ecstasy are ours to enjoy while we may
For they serve to bridge hurts of another day.
My beloved! Have faith from doubt secure,
Have hope that will always endure;
These years that keep swiftly passing by
Serve only our love to purify!
                                        Your Gilbert

The words that Brandon had uttered during their laundry room meeting about his own parents also loomed large in her mind. The shortness of life is not the criteria to measure accomplishments or success as a human being. Those words had extended meaning for her now too.

The Alliance held a special memorial service. Many people attended, most of whom Lucy did not know. There were many who had their future affected in one way or another by Estelle's deeds. Her role as a symbol had led many to do what otherwise might not have ever been done. Lucy's tears were often matched by the genuine tears of many others. Lucy could not bring herself to say anything, but Brandon spoke on her behalf with just the right touch of appreciation for the Posts and for all of those who aided them in the pursuit of righting a world in danger. Even Lucy's grandparents were there. She had not seen them for a good number of years, but there was a sincerity about their embrace that revealed more than words might say. Through her swollen eyes she could still see the agony and the guilt.

Christmas was an especially difficult period. Justin and Estelle had always fussed over this holiday. They went all out with festive touches and special meals. Boxes of sentimental decorations collected over the years were not unpacked this year. No tree where there were at least three spread around the house. No special presents hidden around the house as a carry over from her childhood years. They often enjoyed the hunt more than she did. She would wind up with more school supplies than she knew what to do with, and it soon became a gag for Justin to give her even more.

Lucy and Brandon did not exchange gifts. They spent the holiday in quiet retreat in the undecorated house, allowing Lucy to absorb all the memories of the past and to collectively instill them in her heart. Brandon was sensitive to each sigh, and a muffled sob often broke through the silence that tore at his heart. He felt her loss, and the fondness that he had instantly enjoyed bestowed on her parents added to his own sorrow. He marveled at the depth of Lucy's feelings. His love was fully entrenched. This unexplainable turn of events revealed anew just how much they needed each other.

SEVENTEEN

Even though the Spring semester had just begun, the University let them delay resumption of the teaching tasks for two weeks in order to settle the estate. Forcing them to go through all of the papers and preparing an inventory of the possessions in the house proved to be difficult. Each fragment of Justin's and Estelle's lives confirmed unfulfilled quests and assumptions that more would be done, clashing with the harsh reality. It seemed as if every document, each item, called for a mind to revisit the past.

Lucy was determined to keep the house. This familiar place in which she had spent her whole life was now a monument to her parents. There was no way she could part with it. Knowing just how much his father's albums meant to him, Brandon was fully supportive of this decision. It might add some emotional upheavals, but it would supply a comfort in the long term.

When Brandon had found Justin's laptop, he wondered why he had not taken it with him. Spellbound, he traveled through the contents of Justin's unfinished book. He searched diligently for other material on the desktops and on disks, but what had been done was apparently all that there was. A wonderful story. A captivating idea. He reread it three times, each time finding new treasures in it. Subtle nuances, hidden symbolism. The wrenching emotional saga of attempting to find and regain a lost love.

Lucy started the daunting task of identifying and sorting her mother's computer files and the wealth of hard copy materials spread around her office. Each seemed to give her a fresh perspective and a renewed appreciation for her mother's abilities and devotion to the causes she believed in. Dedication and commitment amply displayed in detailed documentation. It all wove a taut human fabric. Estelle had been a wonderful mother. She had also been a forward-looking thinker and leader. The vision was basic. First, save the world from ravage. Second, preserve with the care and respect its natural components so that the world would have a future.

Back at Blantyre, only the opportunity needed to arise for them to confront the decisions already made and to bring them forth into the light. As they sat huddled together on the sofa, only the gentle ticking of the clocks held the moments together. The impact of the unanticipated event had altered the direction of their lives. Before they actually voiced the inevitable choices, a silent understanding took hold that any unilateral decision would be a mutual commitment. Their love had been pushed well beyond the frivolity of a courtship. There was now an overriding serious commitment to a set of ideals and to each other.

Lucy spoke first. Great comfort in knowing that she did not need to be concerned with how she would phrase her thoughts and how they might spill out. He would judge neither her pronouncement nor how it came out. "As much as this may seem like a rash plan, it is not. At this point, I will be satisfied with nothing less. I want, ... I need .... to pick up where my mother left off. I just know that she would have wanted me to carry on for her in her place. I realize that all my life she has been grooming me for this eventuality. She instilled in me this total commitment to secure and safeguard the environment. Since her death, it is almost as if her drive and determination have been transferred to me. I have already approached the trustees of the Alliance, and they are thrilled to have me take over for her. Not only is there the name recognition, but they feel it would be a great tribute to her and the cause she celebrated. My young age does not seem to be a handicap in the light of these other considerations. They even promise to spare me from the full thrust of fund-raising duties."

She grasped Brandon's hand with a firmness symbolic of her determination, and continued knowing full well that he was attentive. "I told them that I needed to finish out the semester here, and that I would start in June. I will work in spurts at the headquarter offices in New York until I get fully acquainted with all of the inner workings of the AGE foundation, but I will be mostly directing operations from home as my mother did. I will be in charge of my own itinerary. The AGE staff will support me in research and planning just as they did with my mother."

Again she paused to squeeze his hand. "I am sure that you are not fully surprised at this. Only one other item is important. I need you by my side to see this through. You add the strength to my areas of weakness, just as my dad was for her. I am so consumed by my love for you that I cannot even visualize succeeding in any venture without your presence and total support."

Another interruption in her dialogue to caress his cheek. "The death of my parents has solidified two aspects of my being. Their commitment is now mine, and through my love I am committed to you. You do not have to say anything just yet. Think about it. I know neither one of us believes in preordained destiny. Yet, this is a destiny that my will and intellect have shown me as the way to assure that their lives had a meaning. Actually, I would have probably gravitated to this kind of role eventually anyway."

Brandon stood, gently pulling her up from the sofa. Her small frame barely reaching his shoulders. He hugged her with an earnest hold, leaving but one interpretation. His placid tone confirmed such an action. "My sweetheart. I fully understand and support you. Whatever is dealt to us in life, by plan or happenstance, we will face it together. It is a very noble undertaking you are planning, and I just know that your parents would have been as proud of you as I am. You and I are joined for all events, for all hopes, for all dreams. Whatever and wherever this decision takes you, I will be there with you and for you."

They kissed. A long kiss, sealing the joint enterprise. An acceptance of personal fulfillment of the demands of the love of two people who have found the love they relish. For one, a constant new discovery. For the other, the culmination of fragmented aspects finally brought to a cohesive whole.

Sitting back on the sofa, hands entwined, Brandon spoke with renewed gusto. "There is another part of this scenario that gives further impetus to my being a part of your decided course. There is another accomplishment to foster the memory of your parents. The novel that your father was working on has completely intrigued me. Its contents and multiple meanings have absorbed me in such a way that I feel compelled to finish it for him as a testament to his talent and imagination. We found no notes as to where he was planning to take the story, but I would very much like to try and put myself in his place and let it lead me to be the substitute author."

Lucy smiled broadly, one of the rare times she had allowed herself to feel and exhibit a moment of joy. "I think that is wonderful. We will both be carrying out their work, and yet doing it for ourselves as well. I fully support that effort, my darling man."

The turn of events had definitely altered their future. An interesting composite of choice and a thrust of circumstance. The challenges loomed large, especially as they were not yet fully defined.

Brandon looked deeply into those clear blue eyes. A sparkle of youthfulness suddenly glazed over by an impromptu maturity. Fierce determination coupled with a softness of sincere delight. It truly amazed him how much he loved this woman. Investigating and experiencing the depth of love would hopefully enable him to grasp the essence of Justin's fictional character, Donald, and his love for Myra. Introspection, detection, resurrection, and projection.

EIGHTEEN

The school year ended without incident, both Brandon and Lucy managing to complete their tasks in satisfactory fashion even though their full attention and hearts were not in it. Once back at the Post home, circumstances fortified their chosen pathway. The house was fully paid off, there had been some savings, and there was a large life insurance policy that had been taken out on Estelle by the Alliance for which Lucy was the beneficiary. Brandon had some savings and investments. A portion of their teaching salaries remained intact. AGE had agreed to pay Lucy a hefty sum to be the head of the organization. She would work from home with occasional visits to the Alliance headquarters in New York City. An increasingly busy schedule for excursions to places around the globe where AGE might be influential was contemplated.

Even the arrival of Brandon's possessions worked out smoothly. The clocks found new homes in spaces throughout the rooms. The books of Brandon's father found a secure accommodation in the Post library. Lucy was quite pleased with how comfortably the new blended with the old.

A significant emotional setback occurred with the arrival of a strange package from Brandon's contact at the Department of State. When Lucy opened it, her heart sank instantly. It was her mother's locket. The locket that Estelle had determinedly pronounced that she would never take off. The note in the package indicated that it had been removed from a cache taken by the Guatemalan army in a round up of bandits. The inscription on the back of one of the photos in the locket...Justin & Estelle, 1974...led the local authorities working with the United States investigators to ascertain ownership. Lucy clutched it to her heart. After a brief hesitation, she put it around her neck. Another part of her mother to remain with her.

The day of their marriage was truly a special one. Brandon wanted to insure that it would be a day just for them, one to look back on through the years to mark the formal launching of an intertwining as exceptional as the magic that had brought them together. A simple civil ceremony. Brandon authored the exchange of vows.

> *Today, Lucy and Brandon are expressing and enhancing the joining of their hearts. Marriage has been established as the official recognition of the happiness and well-being of a woman and a man. For Lucy and Brandon, the harvest is bountiful. The true riches of their lives will be the comfort and support, physically and emotionally, that they give to each other. Both sets of parents, if they would have lived to know this moment, would have been contented with the abundance of feeling and caring that this couple has found together. This exchange of wedding vows, this joining of woman and man, brings with it all of the beauty of life and the vital forces of nature. To that and to themselves, Lucy and Brandon make this commitment. Brandon, do you take Lucy to be your partner in loving and living? Lucy, do you take Brandon to be your partner in loving and living? May each moment of your lives together be as close and meaningful as the present tender look in your eyes, the warm beating of your hearts, and the joyous sound of your will in harmony that echoes the love you feel. The pronouncement now for the entire world to hear — you are husband and wife.*

A hired chef prepared a gourmet meal for them at the house. Later they camped out amidst the lush bushes in the back. The night was cool and calm, and the stars served as an umbrella to shield them and to contain them. The symbolism accentuated the realism for them that the world harbored within them was as mighty as the universe.

For Lucy it was also a tribute to her parents. Never had she thought that when and if she ever did marry that her parents would not be there to share in the joy. Yet, they were the ones that had made it possible. They had instilled in her the capacity to give and accept love, and to recognize that its true significance was multifaceted. It enhances the smallest of pleasures and curtails the negative impact related to life's pursuits.

It was that night, comforted in the arms of Brandon that Lucy finally absorbed the reality of her parent's deaths. It was the closure that was needed so much. Her life's endeavors would be their accomplishments as well as her own, and the love that she had with Brandon would be the continuation of the legend they had created. Not the legend of Blantyre University and the Post Rebellion. Rather, the perpetual story of togetherness. The ongoing legacy of a love powerful enough to prevail in the face of adversity, tender enough to soothe quivering nerves. The feeling that all deserve to have and that all should aspire to.

Their lovemaking under the stars was as fervent as ever. Physical demands drove them to heightened pleasures. A mental and emotional bundling of recent events and new directions catapulted burgeoning sensations. Cascading delights of flesh, renewing the secret known only by those who love deeply and earnestly. The only true satisfying sex is that which is a manifestation of that kind of love. Physical release is only part of the equation. The heart and mind need satisfaction as well.

NINETEEN

The visit to the New York office of the Alliance for a Green Earth had been delayed for a few days. Lucy was reluctant to leave Brandon, but it was necessary to solidify a relationship with the home office staff and to become acquainted with how that office was managed. Then she might best determine how to use their services and how much she could rely on their talents.

She was warmly greeted by the small and animated office personnel. All seemed genuinely eager to assist her and to make her feel welcome to the AGE family. The plaque on her office, *Lucy Post Weyland,* gave her momentary pause and reflection. Not for one second did she doubt that she could accomplish this job, but she would have liked the added incentive of basking in her mother's pride for the undertaking.

It was then that she was informed that a man had been waiting to see her for two days. He was waiting in the reception area. A rather tall man, not as tall as Brandon, with a gaunt face fragmented by lines emanating from the corner of his deep-set eyes. Slightly stooped at the shoulders, he gave the distinct impression that he had been carrying heavy burdens.

When confronted by Lucy, his expression was one of amazement. "You look so much like your mother," his voice husky and shaky as his gaze riveted on the blue eyes before him. "Forgive me for staring. It is as if the past has caught up with my present. My name is Ted Amherst. I knew your parents at college, but they probably never mentioned me by name."

Lucy, once again not fully prepared for an ensuing event, clasped his outstretched hand. "I am sorry to say that I do not recall the name, but please come into my office. I would like to hear more about them in those early days. They were reluctant to talk about that time at any length, even though they knew it intrigued me."

Once settled in the office, Lucy studied the man sitting across from her. Because of the lines in his face and the thinning hair flecked with gray, it was difficult to determine his age. The glasses he wore had rather thick lenses but could not hide the squinting, dark eyes. What ominous tale was he going to relate to her?

For Ted, it was more of a trying moment than he had anticipated. Before him, separated only by a desk, was Estelle's youthful presence. A woman who so closely resembled the one woman in his life who he had truly loved that it shook him at the very base of his fragile being. He had thought about Estelle so much over the ensuing years and had never stopped loving her or needing her. No other woman who crossed his path could compare with her qualities, or match her dynamic flare for living and for intellectual battle. Of course, he had not fully realized that at the time, and he had been torn apart by too many other expectations for him to realize it and to sort out priorities. His short-term destiny obliterated all reason. Now that he was confronted by such a haunting reminder of his past, the dilemma arose as to how much of it he wanted to face or how much he should convey about it.

Ted cleared his throat and spoke methodically. "I had been an early friend of your mother; later of your father as well. They both made lasting impressions on me. I thought of contacting your mother many times, but since I had not accomplished anything worthy of mention, I always backed off. It was only when I read about them in the newspaper did I realize that I had to come to see you. I just had to tell you how very sorry I am that you have lost them. I lost them in a way as well, long before this. I never did really apologize to them. I never did set the record straight, as I should have. In a strange way, I think they understood. They knew me better than anyone else ever has."

He grew quiet, staring at the floor. Collecting his demons, perhaps. Lucy did not want to press him further. As soon as she spoke, his eyes caught hers and they seemed to hold a tale of their own ready to burst free. "My parents were exceptional people. They were very understanding and tolerant. They knew me very well. More than a parent might understand a child. More as if I was also the personification of humanity under their care and influence. It is only now that I fully realize that it is love that brings the interest, the patience, and the capacity to know all of the intricacies of another human being. I, too, have lost the opportunity of letting them know that I now understand this, how much I appreciated it. It sustained me without my ever knowing it."

It was now Lucy who was staring out in the distance in the direction of the window. It was difficult to hold back the tears. Her thoughts probably matched his as well. Why, oh why, do we not fully appreciate what we have until we have lost it? Without a second thought, she fingered her mother's locket through the thin material of her blouse. The locket had become an integral part of her being, an uninterrupted continuation of her past with her present and her future. The locket symbolized a key to unlock all the doors of opportunity that she might encounter.

As if his trend of thought had righted itself, Ted continued solemnly, "I was the leader of the student revolt at Blantyre in 1974. In hindsight, I am not proud of who I was then and the consequences that others had to bear, particularly your father. All of the blame was heaped on him as the cause of those events. He was teaching a seminar dealing with anarchism, and I was in that class with other student activists. He had nothing to do with the student unrest. Actually, he tried his best to help us understand who we were and where we were in the societal framework. He tried to impress on us that there were other ways, constructive ways, to change the system that seemed so oppressive to us at the time. We listened, and he was very persuasive, but it was too little, too late. The impetus had developed a life of its own, and it escaped from my grasp. He had even convinced me to turn my life in a different direction, but I was too swept up in the role I was playing and what was expected of me. The truth of it is that I enjoyed that sense of power. I loved being in the spotlight. I wanted my words and deeds to prompt others into action. In some warped way, I thought I could make history. The fact was that I was so enamored with it all that under the guise of control I had no control at all, least over myself. Afterwards, I could not adjust to the real world. I have never been satisfied with the ordinary motions of life. I could not hold a job for very long. I resented having a boss. Two marriages have ended in divorce because I could not live within the imposed boundaries of a commitment to another person. I have been floundering all of these years. It is as if everything was anticlimactic. Your parents, who had their feet solidly on the ground, have been the true successes. I should have taken their message more to heart."

Lucy interrupted by compulsion. One of her greatest weaknesses still emerged at inopportune times. "Even though I am young in years, I have garnered some wisdom. Much, I am sure, can be attributed to the closeness of my parents, but I had an interesting experience recently. Ironically, I wound up teaching at Blantyre for a year. I was not making a go of it until my now husband gave me the lift I needed and led me to put everything in perspective. Failure can often be the precursor to success. Attitude is so vital in all we undertake. You have many years in front of you to make up not to my parents for I sense they forged their own alliance, but to show yourself the stuff you are really made out of. My father was an avid student of proverbs, as you probably well know. I would give anything to have him before me spouting one right now. Over my growing years many of them have stuck with me as being so illustrative of life. In a few words they can convey such a depth of meaning. One that comes to mind right now, was one of his favorites, one he had cited often for the rewards of a good attitude. It is from China: *Keep a green tree in your heart, and a song bird will surely come to it."*

"Yes, wise words from such a young lady. The tone and impact so reminiscent of your father's attempts to have me instill the kind of faith in myself, to do what I would really like to have done. But I did not come here for your pity. Rather, I wanted to give you my sympathy for such a great loss."

"I so much appreciate that. Are there any particular memories about my parents that you could share with me?"

Ted wrestled with himself about telling Lucy that he had been her mother's boyfriend before her father entered the picture. Victory came in restraint. It gave him a glimmer of satisfaction to know that he was capable in some small way to do what might be better for someone else than for himself. Not just the coming here to give Lucy his sincere sympathy, but being able to withhold some information that might tarnish Estelle's image for her daughter. Or was it really his image? If he revealed that he had been Estelle's lover, he would also have to tell her that he lost her because he had driven her away from him with the miserable disdain he foisted on her because of her opposition to his leadership and the plans he developed. He would have to admit that he had ignored Estelle's poignant protestations and tolerated her stance only because she was unable to sway any of the students from his yoke.

Lucy watched the slight twitch at the corner of Ted's eye. There was also an evident tremble to his bottom lip as he continued to speak in a voice losing its resonance. "They were very private people. I was so absorbed in my own internal and external conflicts that I probably failed to notice many of the things they did together, even the obvious ones for those very much in love. I do remember, however, that since your father was a teacher and your mother was a student, it was taboo for them to be seen together in any sort of compromising situation. So, instead of meeting on campus, they used to meet in the evenings at a diner off the school grounds. I assume they always thought that they were safe from exposure there because at night the diner was usually empty. They probably never knew that one of the other students in your father's seminar was a dishwasher there a few nights during the week. He kept us all informed of the romantic huddling. Lots of hand-holding, gaga eyes."

Lucy smiled. Ted's description not only transported her mind to a pleasant memory of her parents to hold onto, it reminded her of Brandon and herself. The warmth crept over her entire body.

Ted noted the far-off look in Lucy's large blue eyes. Another look reminiscent of a past best put behind him. He rose, extended his hand towards her's, and shuddered imperceptibly when she grasped it. "I have already taken more of your time than I should have. I'd best be off. There are other loose ends that I need to tie up."

"I am very glad you came by. I very much appreciate your effort and your kind thoughts."

When Ted emerged back on the street, he felt a familiar resolve take hold. He just had to put his life in some kind of manageable order. He had to persevere at some worthwhile endeavor. Now that he had confronted Estelle's ghost, he vowed to do it as a tribute to her. Once more she had done more for him than he had ever done for her.

It took some time for Lucy to settle down to the Alliance tasks at hand. Her surprise visitor had left her mind reeling between the past and the present. She had the distinct impression that Ted had not told her all that he was prepared to tell her. Perhaps there had been some deeper bond between him and one or both of her parents for him to have made such a special trip to see her. It did little to satisfy the curiosity about her parent's courtship. It merely reinforced the notion that their love had prevailed at a difficult period in their lives — a confirmation that love eases the hardships along life's pathway. It was a valuable reminder of what she now had in her life with Brandon.

The leaves of a tree are many, but the root is one
[CHINA].

Sweet are the tears that are dried by your loved one
[PORTUGAL].

*Let love be like drizzle: it comes softly, but still swells
the river*
[MADAGASCAR].

TWENTY

The first day that Brandon had the house to himself, he settled into the writing room hoping that the aura would assist him in resuming Justin's novel. If only he had an inkling of how he had wanted the plot to continue. Was Myra's curt announcement to end communications in earnest? Would Donald merely accept it? Had Justin contemplated an ongoing series of communications between the characters? Would there eventually be a face-to-face meeting? If so, what would that bring on? How might this kind of story end? Could a man throw away his family and the orderly life he had been living to recapture a lost love?

The quiet surroundings only fed his torment further. Looking out on nature's splendor, just as Justin must have done countless times, prompted his mind to race in many directions at once. This was going to prove more difficult than he had originally contemplated.

To calm his raging imagination, and to soothe the growing agitation, Brandon reached for an album and read some of his father's poems. They were a sure anchor to moor the storm-tossed ship of his mind.

> *22nd Anniversary—*
> *Time cannot measure, in overtones or nuances,*
> *The growing radiance and powers*
> *That, like links in a chain of circumstances,*
> *Lift to an exalted plane this love of ours.*
> *Built on foundations of steadfast mutuality,*
> *Despite some shadows amidst sunny contentment,*

Through the medium of comradeship and solidarity,
With spirit undivided, life unfolds resplendent!
To you, my Queen of Grace, my Lady of Delight,
I owe everything I love so much;
The rapture in my heart is but partial insight
To rewards that stem directly from your touch.
                                           Your Gilbert

Thoughts and Sentiments on Our 4th Anniversary—
The pedestal upon which from the first you have rest-
ed
So deservedly and as graceful as a dove
Was designed and created out of soundly tested
Ingredients — the chief of which being my undying
love —
And from that exalted perch and view
You have heard, like clarion bells pealing,
And seen, shimmering as sun flakes on the morning
dew,
The essence, the conviction and thus the believing
That where each wills the other's course,
And counts every moment and contact as ONE,
The triumph of togetherness is the steering force
Meaning that love cannot be undone — only rebegun!
                                           Your Gilbert

Reflections on Our 20th Anniversary—
These twenty years were not required
As a time element in which to react;
Or an interval so arranged and desired
To demonstrate an unalterable fact;
That LOVE is LIFE — timeless like a reverie
Unspent, fluid, never stilled —
An exalted state, in fact and memory,
Keeping its overtones unfailingly distilled;
Surviving forces that interplay
And beat, drum-like, against its face
It is still cumulative in a special way,
Retaining its power, grandeur and grace.

With hearts attuned to this majesty,
Let us rejoice in our status of Man and Wife,
And with hands clasped in an ecstasy,
Implement this truth that Love is Life!
                                    Your Gilbert

By the second day, Brandon was ready to begin writing. He would take the events as they developed, leaving the story and its ending as the product of a free and daring will.

My Dearest Myra —
You should know me well enough that I would not adhere to your last effort to discontinue this contact. You call it a noble act. I do admire your attempt to turn the head of the wild beast, but it is too late to rein in the steed. Dwelling upon your response, it only charms me more and instills in me an even greater admiration for your desire to do the right thing. But we are not involved in a situation where there is any clear right or wrong. My novel is not only a statement of a cause, it has spawned its own consequences. Before, through, and after the book you are now a very real piece of my life. I should give it up as you urge. Yet, whether I can or not is immaterial. I do not want to give it up!

I have looked up the meaning of your name. It is quite appropriate. Myra means "longed-for."

In my years on this Earth, I have learned much, although I am sure there is much more for me to grasp. One thing that I have discovered is that love has enormous potential and can reach great proportions. I love my family. I love my friends. I love my relatives. I love you. Each is loved in a different way. Each love does not exclude the others. So, why should I sacrifice this love I feel for you? It has its distinct, special place in my heart.

You may decide not to respond. You may prefer to ignore me. Yet, for me there is a compelling connection, and I will continue to send these messages. Writing them brings on fulfillment of its own. A combination, perhaps, of a guilty conscience, a rampant imagination, and a dream beyond reasonable expectation of coming true.

Maybe I cast you in a role that transcends human practicality. The writer in me is to blame for that. If I am to conjure up an ideal character, I must bestow those qualities that I would be most satisfied with. I suspect, however, that I am merely reflecting who you really are. That is why your valiant attempt to effectuate what might be "socially" correct merely confirms my appraisal of your being.

So, forgive me for not heeding your overt intent. My messages will now pour forth as my mind and heart spill over. After all, this has brought me to a point well beyond the person I have been and the so-called "normal" or "regular" life that I have lived before. Now that I have tasted the sweet nectar of finding you, I am addicted to it.

Please take my words and emotions as a sincere desire for them to be pleasurable and non-coercive elements in your life. You can relegate it to a tiny part of your life. Please leave a little room for me in your heart.

Lovingly,
Donald

Brandon leaned back in the chair. For a few moments he stared out the large expanse of glass to the mass of green trees on the hillside. This kind of writing was intoxicating. One becomes immersed in the characters. It consumes a great deal of energy and requires dedicated concentration. Since Justin had written two previous books, he may have handled it with greater ease. Brandon knew too well that he would not be able to rest that day until he had fashioned a response by Myra.

It was the very next day that Donald received a reply from Myra. He had to read it three times before its full impact settled into his mind and spirit.

Donald:
You have portrayed me all along as having abnormally high emotional strength. How wrong you are! My greatest weakness is that my heart is too large for my body. I wept when I read your message. Yes, I have tried to do what I thought was the best thing for you. After I sent that note, the regret crept in. It was not the best for me. What

woman can resist such an outpouring of love? What woman, as fragile in spirit as I am, can reject such a love? Being a hopeless romantic, just the thought of my first love being my last love, captures my entire being.

So, now that I have surrendered to your plea, what do we do? Where do we go from here? Do we go back to relive an era? Do we jump ahead and live a new life? Is any or all of this possible? If love is confusion, I am in love.
                                        Myra,
                                        the weak one.

Brandon walked slowly around the room. Undoubtedly, Justin would have done a better job in reaching this point. In a rewrite, he would try to flesh it out. Add a touch here and there. It was extremely satisfying to delineate a story to bring characters to life. Would a reader also find a similar sense of enjoyment? Would one say this cannot possibly be real? Yet, what is reality? Is it not what we can make it to be? In a tale, is it not what we may want it to be?

> *Imagination is the only weapon*
> *in the war against reality*
> [JULES DE GAUTIER].

> *Imagination is more important*
> *than knowledge* [ALBERT EINSTEIN].

> *Reality can be beaten with enough imagination*
> [ANONYMOUS].

TWENTY-ONE

Upon Lucy's return, there was much to catch up on. The daily telephone calls were insufficient to capture and hold the details and full reactions to events while they were apart. Lucy elaborated on Ted Amherst's visit, and the more she thought on it and talked to Brandon about it, the more convinced she was that there had to have been a more intimate story to have been told. Why he had left it unrevealed was his albatross. Lucy sensed all too well that she would never know those details of the past.

Brandon let Lucy read what he had written. She thought it was intriguing, and she definitely thought that Brandon had well emulated her father's writing style. The more she thought about her father's book also raised a specter of a past that she probably would never know. Had the character of Myra been a total figment of his imagination? Had there been a lost love in his life that he had dwelled upon? For as much as she thought she had known her parents so well, there were too many questions emerging that would go unanswered. Not that it really mattered in the total picture. After all, that had been in their past. She was confident that she had shared their lives as the love child. She was comfortable believing the full and honest extent of their love for one another and for the love that they poured over their child.

That night, the pent-up passion was only fully released after an extended period of close contact. An outpouring of the tender words of affection. The touches of inflamed bodies leading to seemingly timeless entries of delight. Being back together was both a celebration and a reaffirmation of their oneness.

Lucy slept late the next morning. She was awakened by quite an unusual event. Was Brandon licking her face? When she opened her eyes, a little fur ball was sitting by her cheek, the possessor of the tiniest, daintiest tongue that was laving her skin. She bolted upright, nearly knocking the animal off the pillow. It was the smallest, cutest puppy that she had ever seen. Brandon stood at the end of the bed. His smile was so broad it appeared to reach almost from ear to ear. "It is a yorkshire terrier, just barely twelve weeks old."

Lucy hugged it, matching Brandon's broad smile. "How did you know I always wanted a dog?"

"When we were going through the papers, I found a note in your father's collection of scribbled notes indicating that you had wanted a dog so badly since you were a little girl and how devastated he had been that because of his allergies he could not give you one. It is another of his undones that I wanted to complete."

"Is it a he or a she?"

"Never thought I would have to give a scientist an anatomy lesson. If you look real closely, you will see that he is a he. Yorkies, as they are commonly referred to, were originally ratters in England. They would be sent into the mines to eliminate the rats. Over the years, of course, they have been bred down in size. This one should not get to be over six pounds. They are lap dogs, so I envision he and I competing to occupy that hospitable place. They hardly shed at all, although they notoriously can be quite yappy. This one seemed especially bright and advanced, as he goes on puppy pads inside or outside to turn the grass yellow. Thus, he is environmentally acclimated. A definite plus I thought for your taking him into your heart."

Lucy gazed upon the small round face, the gleaming dark eyes and the shiny black speck of a nose. "I love him already, and I love you for giving this special present to me. What a wonderful surprise."

"I can see you are bonding already. I wanted you to have another token of my love. This is an animated version."

"Does he have a name?"

"That privilege is all yours."

"Let's see. An ordinary name will not do. It has to be special to recognize that he is ours. Blantyre!"

"A mouthful, but quite appropriate. I thought you might pick some environmental category, such as coral reef or wetland."

In the following weeks, Blantyre wormed his way into their hearts and into their daily routine. He proved playful, spirited and loving. Dog toys accumulated rapidly, as each trip to the store seemed to warrant getting him another item for his amusement. He accompanied them on their long walks, and seemed to have a knack of being carried most of the way. The fur ball was a wonderful source of entertainment and diversion from the more serious matters surrounding them. He displayed the great features of a dog that humans would do well to have — unconditional love and unqualified loyalty and trust. After a month, he was sleeping with them in their bed. He would curl up against Lucy, and it surely must have been his interpretation of doggie heaven. A mutual source of warmth and comfort. During their lovemaking, he would sit still gazing intently at them as if he was wondering why humans would want to engage in such a frantic activity. A matter even more puzzling, no doubt, when they had him fixed.

As the time glided away, the months took on an order and settled routine that was comforting in its own way. Lucy, accompanied by Brandon, made her first representative trip for AGE to San Francisco. They attended two dinner receptions, Lucy gave two detailed speeches, and there were a bevy of visits to local politicians and environmental groups to display affirmative support for environmental issues both on and off the political agendas. Blantyre was left with Mrs. Gordon, a long-time neighbor, widowed for many years. She had been like a grandmother to Lucy, and had taken an instant liking to the fur ball. It promised to be a pleasing regular companionship.

As they relaxed on the return flight, Lucy could not help but think that this must have been the way her parents had been. Working as a team, and leaning on each other. Matching a weakness with a strength. She released Brandon's hand long enough to stroke his cheek. He took her hand and placed his lips to it. A gentle way of saying I love you. A thought in unison. How could I ever be without you?

TWENTY-TWO

Brandon had advanced on the book during this period. Donald and Myra continued to exchange messages, each sharing precious memories of the past and personal thoughts of the moment. Each communication drew them to the ultimate decision that they wanted to see each other. They were predisposed to such a reunion. Their mutual outlook, based on a common foundation, had already brought the meeting to a theoretical occurrence. Now, only the happening of the convergence of the past with the future was needed. Mulling over the possibilities, Brandon finally determined how it would happen.

Donald was quite nervous. Much was riding on this decision. No wonder his stomach was queasy, his lips parched. Once they had decided to meet, the time and place became crucial. He was able to locate an isolated cabin for rent in a State forest. It was furnished and fully stocked with the essentials, and even had a full kitchen and a fireplace. All that he had to do was to bring the food.

As he sat on a step leading to the porch waiting for her, the surroundings were not lost upon him. They had a significance of their own. The only sounds to penetrate the quietude were the wind passing through the pine trees and the warbling of the late summer birds. Autumn was just around the corner and the sugar maples, the first trees to turn color were already flecked with red and yellow.

As he waited, his heart hammered in his chest. A slight chill hovered in the air, but he could feel the dampness in his armpits and there was a clam-

miness in the palms of his hands. A hint of the thrill of a young Donald awaiting his first date penetrated his demeanor. He had no idea how he would react, what he might possibly say that might bridge the intervening years. The growing not shared, the experiences in isolation. Imaginary dialogue seemed quite inadequate for such a momentous reunion. There was an overwhelming sense of anticipation. Finding a lost love has to be a giant first step. Taking hold of it and sustaining it looms even larger. Yet, through their written communications they had renewed their knowing about each other from the inside out. A true advantage to see the inner workings, appreciate the inner beauty, to make the physical appearance much less important.

An hour passed, and he found that his patience did not wear thin. He was that certain that this old love was worthy of such tolerance. A poem that he had stumbled upon in his readings ran through his mind, a poem that he had quoted in the novel:

> Other loves may come to us and will,
> And may hold us in their spell until
> With a half regretful sigh,
> We discover by and by,
> There's a charm about the old love still.
>
> F.W. Vandersloot, There's
> A Charm About the Old Love Still
>   (1901).

The sound of her car on the gravel road pierced his reverie. When it stopped next to his car, he slowly walked towards her as she got out. The years had been kind to her. She was wearing a white blouse and navy shorts. Her figure was still slim, her legs shapely. The short wavy hair was still the same light brown color, and the skin on her face as yet youthfully taut. A red glow appeared on her cheeks, the blush emblem of the childhood years reemerging. A seductive grin revealed teeth glistening with apparent care.

Without any hesitation, they were in each other's arms, hugging. So familiar, so natural. They kissed deeply, again reminiscent of a time when such was a constant act of devotion. As they parted, the sweetness remained on their lips, the honey in their souls. Another kiss, filled with a tender passion that neither had experienced for a long time. A young love cascading to the forefront.

They stared intently into one another's eyes, reading the most important message of their reattachment. It was a scintillating moment. The intervening years had vanished in an instant. There were no other people in the world, or any other life beyond this place and time.

Myra was the first to speak. Her voice was as full and soft as he had remembered it, as he had dreamed it was. "Well, you must have been saving this up. Am I in Heaven?"

"Heaven is anywhere you want it to be. You used to bring out the best in me, and I think you are back to your old tricks."

Her laughter so freely offered was as hearty as he recalled it to be. "It is not my trick. You are the magician."

Hand-in-hand, they strolled through the woods. Even the entwined fingers had the comfort of a regularly employed action. They stopped often to embrace and kiss, filling the coffers of their unity.

That night, as naked bodies melded, the flames of a young love ignited anew. It carried them to great heights. Just as they had discovered their bodies and sensuality as youngsters, the journey was not new but never more exciting. Added to the delight was the firmness of their conviction that this was right for them. Long after repeated peaks of sexuality, they lay in each other's arms with as much of their bodies in contact as possible. Myra whispered in his ear, "Dearest one, you may not recall this, but the very first time we kissed, I told you that I thought it was remarkable how our bodies fit together so well. It might just as well have been yesterday, because we are still a perfect fit. That alone is so reassuring to me."

The following three days further illustrated loving compatibility. The lovemaking was fervent, emotional outpouring constant, and the conversation totally committed to themselves and the here and now. It was filled with the promises of forever.

Donald looked deep into those pensive brown eyes. "As I think back on our early days, I dare say there was no subject we left undissected."

"Yes, we sure dabbled as amateur philosophers. Gutter wise and street foolish. I think I liked it best when we discussed the meaning of life."

"I am not sure about you, but I have not made any great inroads from those early observations."

"Neither have I. I probably have fallen behind. Back then we at least had the fresh perspective of youthful innocence. Speaking for myself, my outlook is now quite jaded."

"Mine, too. I probably know more about it now but certainly understand it less."

They were sitting together on a large flat rock, looking onto a field of wild-flowers that had just begun to whither. A symbolism to grasp.

Donald continued, his voice full with the greater significance of the moment as they shared thoughts to match the extent of their emotions. "No matter how one slices it ....LIFE is a four-letter word."

Her chuckle was genuinely warm. "We have always indulged in a profusion of four-letter words."

"I don't suppose you mean those curse words that we avoided as being so crass. Rather such words as love, home, work, mind, idea, care, song, and the big one ..... cash."

"Don't forget the other giant.....death."

"Hey, that is five letters."

"When you are in love, investigating the intricacies of life, what's one little letter more or less?"

It was his turn to chuckle. "Proof positive that I can count on you even if your counting process needs some improvement."

"Ah, but I have your number as well. So, now let's cut to the chase. What do you now think is the meaning of life?"

"I suppose the truest response is that there is no certain or well-defined meaning. It has, or can have a different meaning for each person. In effect, I guess we either make our own meaning and try to live up to it, or we live it first and then try to explain it as some reasonable pattern or model. Often, it probably defies actual description. If one is lucky enough to find it and recognize it as such, then the essence is known. And for you?"

"I echo your portrayal. Yet, I think it is very elusive. There can be so many elements, distant and unconnected, that rather than finding a meaning we compromise with the elements that we can take hold of and can live with. It may even rise to the surreal in the sense that it may not be as it is but what we would like it to be."

Donald took hold of her hand, tenderly massaging the slender fingers. Myra had always been a special person. What they had was also very special. It was unique because they had not been like others. Perhaps they had fit the stereotype of young lovers, but there were so many attributes that were theirs alone. The intervening years had apparently not altered that, and the recaptured love convinced him that the wrong he had done was now truly righted. She had been his best friend. She still was.

Her lips grazed his hand, and she looked at him longingly. "There must be another subject we can now talk to miniscule proportions."

His grin broadened as he gazed upon this person who mysteriously had been such a paramount part of his life, and now had retaken that posture with so little effort. "I am sure they will emerge as we plod ahead. It is just baffling to me how the paths people travel can cross, and then at some distant point in the journey they can converge. With all of the people in the world, with all of the possibilities, it is staggering to the mind how lives that should intersect do so."

"I knew that you would get into a different subject........destiny. Are things meant to happen, or are there just a set of circumstances that play havoc with our lives? In my travels I have found that one of the things most difficult to discuss with people is whether an event, for good or for evil, was bound to happen or whether it just happened. Was it preordained or chance? Worse yet as a concept, but one which I can readily understand as a matter of comfort or conscience, that something did not happen because it was not meant to happen. From this comes the subjective rationalization that it did not happen because it means that there is something better to happen down the road."

"Not to mention the further belief that one has no control over his or her destiny. There is another that pulls the strings."

"Not to mention the additional perplexity that when an event happens it can be interpreted in so many ways, often influenced by other events and other persons."

They peered over the tops of the wildflowers gently waving in the breeze. The answers were not out there to be discovered. One must look inside for guidance. Just as they knew that the answers for them now lay with them, with their resolve to be together and to make it work.

Thereafter, Brandon worked on the book feverishly until it was finished.

MEMORY HAVEN
by Justin Post with Brandon Weyland

He had tossed around the idea of two endings. One for the romantics to satisfy the capture of a lost love and for reestablishing it as a total, fulfilling romance. The other where Donald would eventually turn his back on the moment of passion and return to and complete his familial role. He opted for the romantic ending after discussing it at length with Lucy. After all, this was a work of fiction, and while the outcome might not have a complete ring of realism or sensibility, and even might be considered a fairy tale by some readers, it was consistent with Justin's philosophy so firmly engrained throughout his second book. There should be no limits for the human experience. As unrealistic as the goals may seem to be, no matter how much society might frown upon and attempt to dissuade such an exercise of free will, as long as it is not unlawful and is deemed right for that individual, then such is worthy of the effort to achieve it. Justin's theme line, often repeated, is that only if one sets goals extremely high can a person reach as high a degree of fulfillment as possible. Only then can the dream possibly come true.

> *Ambition is our idol, on whose wings*
> *Great minds are carry'd only to extreme;*
> *To be sublimely great, or to be nothing.*
> SOUTHERNE, *The Loyal Brother*

> *That like I best that flies beyond my reach.*
> MARLOWE, *The Massacre at Paris*

> *Dreams are true while they last,*
> *and do we not live in dreams?*
> TENNYSON, *THE HIGHER PANTHEISM*

TWENTY-THREE

Justin's publisher agreed to publish the book, although the company did not ordinarily publish works of fiction. The President and Vice President of the publishing company were of the opinion that Justin Post's books had been profitable enough for them over the years that they were obliged to publish it. However, there was a minimum print run, and a definite lack of enthusiasm on the marketing end. No book reviewer picked up on it. Between these business realities and the fact that it probably had an appeal only to a limited group of potential readers, sales were minimal and the book languished on many a shelf. Yet, for Brandon and Lucy it was not necessary for it to be a commercial success. It was the completion of a special commitment. It had brought the culmination to an emotional and intellectual undertaking that Justin had started. It was their personal tribute to a man who deserved to be honored in whatever way possible.

In its wake, the task had left Brandon somewhat drained. He was sure that he would not undertake writing any more fiction. In the back of his mind over the years was to work on several books on international law, and he had a feeling that he would be able to adapt to that kind of project with greater ease since there were set boundaries for the subject matter and academic research was the mechanism to that end. Fiction writing is a wild ride of emotions and thought patterns. Confusion and conflict adhere in the attempt to absorb the role of each character. Sensitivities and varying temperaments of an assortment of personalities fray the nerves and test the patience. Then, having to mesh the individuals to the story line takes exceptional concentration and maximum effort, even in a book such as

Memory Haven where the thread of the story was rather straightforward. Imagine if it had been a real story within a story, and even some novels have three or four stories running simultaneously.

He was able to regain most of his intellectual composure by becoming an adjunct faculty member at the local college. It was nearby, and the hours were not so demanding that he could not still assist Lucy with her mammoth undertaking. The two political science courses he began teaching were well within his training and experience, one being on American Government and the other on the Conduct of Foreign Affairs.

Then, of course, there was the settling of his soul in the love for and with Lucy. She not only became a pillar of strength in the carrying out of her objectives at AGE, but there was also a total absorption as his mate. Their compatibility was a constant and consistent source of amazement to him. Ranging from the fierce fires blazing in the lovemaking to the tenderest of touches or clasp of hands, there was the serene sense of unity of will and purpose. Even the slight chuckle each time they passed a laundromat sparked a keen feeling of togetherness. Cogent moments built on sweet memories adding grace and strength to their edifice of love.

Topping off the return to order was the renewed appreciation of his father's poems. He used to read them for the pleasure of the thoughts and language. Now, they were the legend alongside the history of Estelle and Justin. All were the bedrock upon which their union was built. So, even now, when Lucy was off on one of her trips to the AGE home office, he settled back in his favorite chair, opened an album and read some of those delicious tidbits. His father's life flowing into his own.

FIRST ANNIVERSARY
From the dreamy dawn of just a year,
Our marital bliss has found no peer;
Through many a heavenly, breathless day
It marched in glory, on and away,
To reach a pinnacle conceived
From the depths of a love conceived
In suffering, tears and despair,
Soared like a graceful bird of the air.
Above the sordid, nebulous, human portals
To join the dwellings of fated immortals.
Surely no promise of the past, flushed
With the fever of burning hope uncrushed,

Was ever more radiantly fulfilled;
No dream divine in any soul instilled
Was ever more completely consummated,
No spirit of sustenance more animated,
No brighter future more definitely intimated.
My ardent wish at this time expressed
Is that another year will see impressed
More deeply and consciously into our lives
These sentiments, which Fate's sharpest knives
Can never mar or quite annihilate –
For all to see, to wonder and to emulate!
                                        Your Gilbert

17TH ANNIVERSARY
The visions of a lover, in terms of time and space,
Are fulfilled with unique and eminent grace
When you, my dear, play the leading role,
Weaving all the little bits into a splendid whole;
To gain a place where, I am proud to say,
You've earned the laurels that you wear this day.

My role, in passing, I would say
Is attending you by night and day;
To care and cherish as long as I live
To render unto you all that I have to give –
A lover in whose worshipful constancy
Your trust and faith may stay eternally!
                                        Your Gilbert

A THOUGHT
Apropos of an overflowing heart –
The days in their routine processional
May not herald events sensational,
Or bring news of a nature climactical;
But one thing is sure
And can be measured by a rule –
The growth of my love is quite mathematical!
                                        Your Gilbert

Brandon closed the album and let it rest on his lap next to Blantyre's sleeping form. Proud to be his father's son, and confident that the best was yet to come.

TWENTY-FOUR

Three years later, a daughter entered the world with a flourish. On Thanksgiving day, Brandon rushed Lucy to the hospital, and within four hours ESTELLE THERESA WEYLAND arrived to add even greater joy to their lives. Theresa was the name of Brandon's mother, and it seemed so appropriate that this new life accentuate the names of both mothers.

Lucy had maintained her demanding schedule right through the eighth month of her pregnancy. She would not let something so spectacular to sway her from her mission except for the briefest period of time. Three weeks after the birth, she was back in full gear. The baby was a delight, and Brandon took to being a daddy as a duck takes to water. He no longer accompanied Lucy on the trips, and was a happy stay-at-home parent. Whenever he had to leave for a class, Mrs. Gordon readily came over to care for the baby and watch over Blantyre. As she was as close to a grandmother to Lucy, the repetitive role for Estelle Theresa was readily and cheerfully accepted.

As for Blantyre, one would think that the baby was his. His greatest joy appeared to be the curling up of his body next to Estelle for their mutual naps. Estelle undoubtedly thought the dog was a toy, and she giggled each time the fur ball licked her cheek.

Fifteen months later, their second daughter arrived to add an even greater measure of happiness to the home and marriage. JUSTINE GILBERTA WEYLAND, named for the fathers, made the family a complete and endearing unit. Blantyre had to share his time with both infants, but it was a challenge he gladly met. Lucy and Brandon were ecstatic, and their arms for embraces elongated to fold in and hold on to the precious additions. Even Mrs. Gordon was looking forward to the expanded challenge.

With Brandon's efforts and devotion to the children, Lucy barely had to break stride in her dedication to her agenda. She was having great success in accomplishing what she had set out to do. She was instrumental in networking with environmental groups worldwide so her actions could have a greater impact. In fact, she had gained such great notoriety that she had been approached to enter the political arena. She would have no part of that, however, and there was no desire to do anything other than her present endeavor. Also, she did not want to get involved in any type of other activity that might detract from her time with the family. Brandon and the girls were the lifeline of her existence.

The wonderful family times abounded as the girls grew into toddlers. Lucy recaptured her growing years. Many of the same warm and memorable activities that she engaged in with her parents were both familiar and new at the same time. There were many walks through trails already established as well as new ones whenever adventure called. There was singing, emanating from happy and eager hearts. The girls quickly took to the favorite of Lucy's childhood.....*The Desperado.* They especially enjoyed the chorus:

There was a desperado
From way down in Colorado,
And he rode around like a big tornado.
He wore a big sombrero
And two guns beneath his vest,
And everywhere he went he gave his war whoop.
WHOOP

They would let out a big whoop, competing to see who could whoop the loudest. In fact, at the end of each chorus there was a renewed opportunity to let out a hardy whoop. Lucy had a slight pang at the word and connotation of a desperado, but it was overshadowed by the sheer joy the girls had in singing it. And there were the reading times. Lucy and Brandon would often read stories aloud together, each taking a different voice in the dialogues. Then there were the extra special activities, such as hayrides, apple and peach picking, and sundry other family outings that kept them learning and laughing. Holidays became extra special times.

Even using the Christmas decorations of her childhood took on added meaning, and it would have been as her parents would have liked it. In each undertaking, there was plenty of laughter, and it was almost as if the girls were uncanny in prompting the parental fussing to increase. Of course, Lucy and Brandon did not put up much resistance.

Brandon made an extra effort to do special activities with the girls when Lucy was away on a trip. Day trips were a common way of introducing them to new vistas, new experiences. Each creating a memory to hold on to. Most of these times were shared with Blantyre, and the girls doted on him. When mommy returned, that always called for a big celebration. They would bake a cake, and make crayon signs showing her the way to the rooms in the house or to where the cake was hidden. Lucy would giggle with gusto, and the girls would chime in with peels of laughter.

As soon as the girls were old enough to start school, the plan was to start Lucy's trips with the family at her side. She looked forward to that. She remembered how she had accompanied her parents on such trips. They were very meaningful not only for what she was exposed to, but it had always given her that secure feeling that her parents wanted her to be with them. It was important that the girls also would have that feeling of unity.

Perhaps life does run in cycles after all. The pattern she had experienced with her parents was now being repeated with her own children. Proving, as if she needed that kind of proof, that the love and influence by parents to a child can be pervasive. Parents can be the greatest role models for children. Lucy and Brandon had both experienced that from the child's end and were now fully exposed to the other end of the truism. So as each new learning and loving experience bolstered the growing of the girls and their attachment to them, all endeavors were further enriched.

> *To understand your parents' love, you must raise children yourself.* [CHINA]
>
> *Children are the reward of life.* [CONGO]
>
> *Children have more need of models than critics.* [FRANCE]

In the study was a small framed 1857 saying stitched on fabric that Lucy's mother and father had pointed to numerous times as their motto in raising her. It seemed just as appropriate as a guideline for Estelle and Justine.

> *The two lasting bequests we can give our children;*
> *one is roots, the other is wings.*

TWENTY-FIVE

Each individual arrives at a crucial point in life that is truly a place of clear self-discovery. This moment of enlightenment may be at a time and place least anticipated, and it may even be in such a subtle form that it demands extra effort to glean its precise significance. Above all, one must be receptive to its arrival.

For Lucy, this special and meaningful moment arrived one otherwise ordinary evening. She had returned from one of her successful missions. Brandon and the girls had picked her up at the airport as usual, fussing over her return with an abundance of affection and stories of their activities in her absence. Estelle was six years old, and Justine had just turned five. It was after eight o'clock in the evening by the time they had arrived back at the house, decorated as expected with the girls' hand-colored signs of welcome and directions to the cake they baked for her. Lucy had started to unpack and catch up on some of the mail and other correspondence piled on her desk. Brandon went off to get the girls ready for bed.

The house was quiet, and Lucy was in a pensive mood. She left the study and went to the living room. As she stood in the doorway, Brandon was lying on the floor on his back, his head propped up on the sofa. He was sound asleep. Curled up in his arms were Estelle on one side and Justine on the other, both also in a deep slumber. Blantyre was stretched out over Brandon's knees as well in a comfortable, warm sleep. An album of Brandon's father's poems was open on Brandon's stomach. He had evidently been reading the poems aloud to the girls. In the course of the relaxing event, all had drifted off to sleep.

Gazing upon this tender scene, Lucy could not help but realize that her life had been a series of doors not knowing what lay behind them. A door never opened is an opportunity lost. So, with resolve she had opened each one in turn eager to confront the challenge that might be there. Surely, everything worth having in life has some risk involved in the search for it. Yet, to not take any and all available chances to attain them can haunt a person for an entire lifetime. She recalled the prophetic words of Helen Kellor that she had read some years back:

> When one door of happiness closes, another opens; but often we look so long at the closed door that we do not see the one which has opened for us.

The sage words in the closing chapter of her father's book also emerged in her mind. She had read them so often they were committed to her memory:

> There is more to being an individual than merely having a different name or an unusual face. There is more to it than conforming to an assigned role in the life play. The scope of the mind's direction and expanse is inviting. There is some mysterious force within and between people that makes each of us uniquely human.

Her father's vital and insightful theory was that even though we do live in a world we never made, we do not have to accept it as it is. We can work with and for others to change it. And then he added the words that had always held great significance for Lucy:

> There is also the possibility of making a special place within it just for ourselves. A warm, inviting niche to allow us to think without limitation, to exist without inhibitions, to exist without criticism or rebuke by others. A space reserved for the inner self to rise to the surface and to elevate to a plateau from which all can be observed and understood without

outside influences. A safe, secure and
congenial mental and emotional fortress.
A place called home.

Gazing upon the slumbering figures before her, Lucy sighed. This was her niche. This was the vital factor of her being. The ultimate love between a man and a woman, the grand delight in loving a child and the child returning that love, all in the home of her birth and the incubation of the love with Brandon and the creation of Estelle and Justine.

Family faces are magic mirrors.
Looking at people who belong
to us, we see the past, present and future.
GAIL LUMET BUCKLEY

Lucy smiled. Silently, she moved over and lay next to her sleeping family. Her arms encircled the group. Her heart embraced the meaning of the moment.